KING ARTHUR
Stories of the Knights of the Round Table

KING ARTHUR
Stories of the Knights of the Round Table

Retold by
VLADIMÍR HULPACH
Illustrated by
JAN ČERNÝ

HAMLYN

First published 1989
Designed and produced by Artia for
The Hamlyn Publishing Group Limited,
Michelin House, 81 Fulham Road,
London SW3 6RB
© Artia, Prague 1988
© This edition by
The Hamlyn Publishing Group Limited 1989
Translated by Vladimír Vařecha
Graphic design by Miroslav Habr

ISBN 0 600 55844 4
Printed in Czechoslovakia by Svoboda, Prague
1/23/02/51-01

CONTENTS

TALE ONE . . .
IN THE VERY
BEGINNING . . .

It all begins with the Trojan War. The fugitive Aeneas becomes the founder of the Roman nation and his great-grandson, Brutus, is exiled. The prophecy of the goddess Artemis and the voyage to the promised island. The Trojans land, and call their new home Britain.

Troy was burning. The mounds, the walls, and the gilded beams of the castle, where proud kings had reigned for centuries, were crumbling and falling. And it was here, in the country we now know as Turkey, that our tales have their very beginning . . .

The victory-drunk Greeks ran through the streets, taking women and children captive to drag them off into slavery and killing the last gallant defenders. The giant wooden horse inside whose frame the Greeks had entered the city, towered like a grim phantom of death over the soulless bodies of the warriors, and over the fires and the rivers of blood.

None of the Trojan heroes had survived. The brave Hector and his forty-nine brothers were slain, as was their father, the aged King, Priam.

However, Aeneas — son of the goddess Aphrodite and the Trojan prince Anchises — did escape and he made

his way to the foot of Mount Ida, where he met up with other fugitives.

What could a fugitive do, in those days, when Fate had decided that he should not die in battle? Just wander around the world, in quest of a new home! . . .

Thus Aeneas had ships built and, with his father and his own small son, Ascanius, he and the other fugitives sailed out into the open seas . . .

After many years and much adventure, the remnants of Aeneas's fleet reached the River Tiber, and it was here that Aeneas was favoured by fortune, when King Latinus gave him his daughter Lavinia in marriage. Fate had decided that Aeneas would be the founder of the powerful Roman nation.

When Aeneas died, Ascanius was elected King. He, in turn, was suc-

10

ceeded by his own son, Silvius. Silvius, too, had a son and he was named Brutus. It was the destiny of Brutus to found Britain . . .

At the age of fifteen, Brutus, in a tragic accident, killed his father with an arrow when they were out hunting. Angered relatives drove the youth out of the country.

Brutus found refuge in Greece where he met many descendants of the vanquished Trojans. He led them out of servitude and, after a victorious battle against the Greeks, he ordered three hundred and twenty ships to be built and loaded with corn. And aboard those ships the Trojans left Greece.

After sailing for two days, Brutus reached a deserted island called Leogetia. He sent three hundred men ashore to replenish supplies and they

discovered, in the middle of the forest, a temple dedicated to the goddess Artemis.

"Offer a sacrifice to the goddess, and ask her which way we are to sail," the Trojans urged Brutus, for it was known that the goddess answered every question put to her by one who had honoured her.

So Brutus took thirteen of his senior men to the temple, and there they made three sacred fires. These were in honour of Zeus, his son Hermes, and his daughter Artemis.

Then, Brutus stepped in front of the goddess's altar, holding an amphora of wine and hind's blood and asked, "Let me know, mighty protector of the

12

young, lady of the moon, ruler of the hunt, which way we are to turn. Tell me where we are to found towns and temples in your honour."

Brutus repeated his prayer nine times, then he walked around the altar four times, sprinkling the wine and blood as he went. Finally, he lay down in front of the goddess's statue, on the hide of the slaughtered hind, and fell asleep.

Artemis spoke to him as he slept. "Sail towards sunset, Brutus," she told him. "When you have passed the distant empire of the Gauls you will see a great isle. There your descendants will build a new Troy, upon which the whole world will look with honour and esteem . . ."

And so the ships set sail westward. After a stormy voyage, the Trojans landed in Mauretania, which we now call Morocco. Here Brutus met a fellow Trojan, named Corineus, whose forefathers had barely escaped with their lives, at the Pillars of Hercules. Corineus was a man of giant strength and he and his followers joined Brutus on his further travels.

The fleet eventually reached Aquitaine, in the south-west of Gaul, where King Goffar was the ruler. He immediately sent his messengers to find out whether the uninvited visitors were bringing peace or war.

Unfortunately, the deputation was led by a man called Himbert, who was strong and quick-tempered, just as was Corineus. Himbert saw Corineus killing a boar with his spear, and he cried, "Who has given you permission to kill the royal game?" Corineus only laughed. "I need no permission!" he answered.

This made Himbert very angry. He set an arrow to the string of his bow, but before he could take aim, Corineus leapt to his side and chopped off his head. Now the Trojans were involved in battle and although the odds were heavily against them, their courage took them to victory. Corineus, in particular, fought like a lion. When he lost his sword in the fighting, he seized his battle-axe with both hands and, with each blow, sowed such terror in the enemies' ranks that they were quickly on the run.

The battle was soon over and the Trojans, having loaded their ships with rich booty, made for the open sea. A favourable wind was blowing and they became greatly excited at the prospect of reaching their new home. Brutus was, perhaps, the most nervous of all. So far everything that Artemis had foretold had come to pass. He hoped she had not altered her divine decision . . . Then, amidst all the uncertainty, he suddenly saw a narrow strip of land emerging from the mist. And, as they drew nearer, he could distinguish cliffs, then trees and shrubs. "Troy Novant! A new Troy!" shouted Brutus.

"Britain!" cried the Trojans, in honour of their leader. The goddess's prophecy had come to pass; the exiles from Troy had found their promised isle. The place where they landed came to be called Totnes and, if you visit that small town today, you may see the Brutus Stone, which marks the actual spot!

TALE TWO...
ENTER MERLIN...

The island called Britain. How Corineus overcomes the giant Gogmagog and how the island is divided after Brutus's death. Constantine dies and power is seized by the tyrant, Vortigern. The building of Vortigern's castle. The mysterious boy Merlin makes the first of his prophecies.

The isle to which the Trojans had been sent by Artemis, and which they named after Brutus, proved to be a truly promised land.

Its soil was fertile and suited the seed-corn they had brought with them and the wooded hills and knolls abounded in game. There were beautiful green pastures and, on the hill and mountain slopes, there was heathland that provided abundant food for the honey-bees. The rivers and lakes teemed with fish.

Like three arms, the rivers later to be called the Thames, the Severn and the Humber, divided Britain into three regions.

At first the Britons, as Brutus's people came to call themselves, believed the island to be deserted, but they were soon to discover otherwise. The caves along the coast were hiding-places for giants, up to four metres tall.

They abounded particularly in the
south-western tip of the island, where
Corineus had settled, and which he
called Cornwall, after himself.

The giants plagued the colonists and
woe to any man they caught alone!
Only Corineus was unafraid of them.
On the contrary, he looked forward to
overcoming the strongest — a giant
called Gogmagog — in contest.

It took some time for the Britons to

fight and kill the whole of the giant population, except for Gogmagog, who was spared to give Corineus the chance to fight him.

And it was a real contest; a rare one to see. Both adversaries panted for breath; Gogmagog tramped upon the ground till the earth shook under him. Then, as they clinched, the giant squeezed his opponent so violently that he broke three of his ribs. The pain gave Corineus a tremendous strength. He seized Gogmagog and, hoisting him up on his shoulders like a sack, he ran towards the sea.

Only when he reached the highest cliff did he stop. And before the giant knew what was happening, he was flying down the rockface like some gigantic boulder. He crashed to the ground and broke into a thousand pieces . . .

After their defeat of the giants, the Britons were able to build their new houses and settlements undisturbed. During Brutus's lifetime, a town that was later to be called London was built on the Thames.

After Brutus's death dominion over the whole island was divided among his three sons. The eldest, Logrinus, received the largest, southern part; he called this Logres. The second son, Camber, began to rule the territory west of the River Severn and before long this came to be called Cambria. The youngest, Albanact, inherited the entire northern part of the island which was called Albany . . .

The centuries passed. The first furrows yielded fertile fields, herds appeared in the meadows, and the forests resounded more and more with the hunters' calls. As well as houses, there were strongholds with palisades around them, for there were many in those rough times who coveted other people's property and might try to acquire it by the sword.

Often, enemy warships would land on the island shores intent on conquering the Britons. But these were unsuccessful, that is until the arrival of Julius Caesar who did coerce the islanders into obedience; not by force of arms, however, but by negotiation. Destiny had decreed that Aeneas's descendants would meet together once again!

Further centuries passed and, as the fifth in our era drew to its close, King Constantine was dying in Britain.

He had three sons, but it was no easy matter to determine which was to succeed him. Both Aurelius Ambrosius and Uther were as yet young boys; the eldest son, Constans, was a monk. Constans had no wish to become a ruler, not being in the least interested in worldly power. But in the end, at the recommendation of Vortigern, the royal counsellor, and also to please his dying father, Constans agreed to accept the crown.

However, Vortigern was not as concerned with the welfare of the young King as it might have appeared. He

himself wanted the throne and, since Constans trusted him, it was easy for Vortigern to take control of some important towns. Then, helped by the Picts who had settled Albany and were threatening the Britons, he had Constans murdered . . .

Now Vortigern was free to proclaim himself King. Constans' brothers were still no threat to him and, to gain the favour of the Britons, he turned his forces against the Picts who had

helped him. However, Vortigern did not enjoy his power for long. Since he oppressed both the nobles and the common people, he had no friends — and the Britons became more and more rebellious.

So he called in the Saxons who had, until recently, made forays against the island and were its arch-enemies; he even gave his own daughter in marriage to their leader, Hengest.

Not even that brought safety to the

tyrant, so he decided to have a stone castle built; only strong and impregnable bastions could save him from danger now!

He chose a suitable site in Cambria, gathered together all the stone-workers in the land, and ordered them to build a castle for him.

No sooner had they started building the tower than, that very night, the walls tumbled down. They built again, and the next night, down tumbled the walls. Vortigern was very angry and supervised the building himself, but to no avail; each morning, instead of walls there was nothing but ruins wherever he looked.

He consulted the royal astrologers

and wise men. "Fate will not have you build the castle in the normal manner," they told him. "Therefore you must find a boy in the land who has no father. Let his blood be mixed with the mortar, and your castle will stand for ever!"

Vortigern was surprised at the advice but, nevertheless he sent out his men into all parts of the country to look for such a boy.

For a long time they searched without success. Then they learnt of a boy living in Carmarthen, whose mother was a simple country wench and who had been fathered by an invisible demon. The demon's evil powers had been cleansed from the infant by the blessing of a priest but it was said that the boy's supernatural powers had been preserved . . .

"He is the right one," said the heralds. They sat him on a horse, and brought him to Vortigern.

The King was delighted, so he gave his young guest food and drink to his heart's content and then asked him, quite kindly, "What is your name?"

"My name is Merlin, and I know why I have been brought here," the boy answered. "But your counsellors are fools. Even if you shed my blood and mix it with the mortar, you will not build the castle. Why don't you ask them what is underneath the site you have chosen?"

Vortigern's eyes almost popped with surprise, yet he did call the wise men

and put the boy's question to them.

They looked at one another in embarrassment, shrugging their shoulders, until Merlin said, "There is a small lake right under the foundations; that is why every wall will fall down!"

And when they dug under the foundations, a small lake was indeed found.

"What now?" asked the boy and the oldest of the counsellors replied, "Well, just drain the lake!" But Merlin laughed. "No, that is not enough, there are two dragons sleeping under it!"

However, Vortigern had the lake drained, and he found that, once again, Merlin was right. There were two caves at the bottom of the lake. After a while a white dragon crawled from one cave and a red dragon from the other, and very soon they engaged in a life-and-death struggle. They belched fire at each other and fought so savagely with giant claws that the lake was filled with their blood. The onlookers' ears rang with their roaring. At first the struggle was not decisive, but gradually the white dragon drove the red one to the shore and seemed to be wearing him down.

The spectators fell back in terror; only Merlin stood motionless, whispering something under his breath.

Then the red dragon recovered; he raised himself on his hind legs and struck the white dragon with such terrific force that he half drove him into the mud. And then a roaring, red flame from the dragon's mouth filled the air . . . Night came, but the fight went on.

Step by step the white dragon retreated before the red one as he was dealt more and more deadly blows. At last both dragons disappeared in the darkness, out of the onlookers' sight; a moment later their roars died down.

Vortigern, still trembling with horror, asked Merlin, "What is all this supposed to mean? You are sure to have an explanation, since you have managed to put even the royal advisers to shame with your powers."

And then the boy Merlin made the first of his famous and well-chronicled prophecies:

. . . Know then, Sire, that you shall not escape a just retribution! With the help of enemies, the Picts and the Saxons, you gained the Royal Crown and harried the British people till they nearly perished.

In such a way, to begin with, the white dragon dominated the red one; but he did not overcome him. You saw how the red dragon, though already exhausted, suddenly put up resistance and with terrible blows and flames retaliated against the enemy, till they were both swallowed up by the darkness.

So, shall you never triumph. For already, the King's sons, Aurelius Ambrosius and Uther, have set sail from Little Britain with many warriors to overthrow you.

A strong castle will not save you. Britons will lay siege to it and burn it down, just as the white dragon was burnt. Hengest with his Saxons will not save you. The Britons will triumph over them just as the red dragon has triumphed.

Then, oaks will blossom again in

Cornwall, and laughter will again resound in Cambria, and the whole island will once more commemorate the name of Brutus. For the foreigners, as well as the names they have given this island, will become forgotten . . .

TALE THREE...
THE BIRTH
OF ARTHUR...

Vortigern falls and Aurelius Ambrosius becomes King. Battles with the Saxons. Eopa poisons Aurelius and a heavenly sign appears. The new King, Uther Pendragon, wishes to make his peace with the Duke of Tintagel, but instead falls in love with the Lady Igraine. Merlin helps the King to achieve his desire. Arthur is born.

Dawn broke over the island and, on the very same day, Merlin's prophecy was fulfilled: Aurelius Ambrosius and Uther landed on the coast with a powerful army.

They landed unopposed. Vortigern sent Britons to fight them, but in vain. Large numbers joined the side of the two true-born Kings and, wherever they could, they took the Saxons — the last of the tyrant's allies — by storm.

Aurelius Ambrosius, who commanded the troops, then decided he must hunt down Vortigern and avenge his brother's death.

For miles and miles the tyrant fled with his faithful few and it was only at Genorea Castle, near Monmouth, that he halted. This was a strong castle, perhaps even stronger than the one he had attempted to build, and when the

Britons laid siege, Vortigern found it easy to defend.

Then, at last, someone recalled Merlin's prophecy: nothing but fire would bring the castle down! The Britons put pitch and bundles of straw under the palisades and set fire to them. At that moment a strong wind blew up; it was so powerful that within minutes the whole castle was ablaze. The gale was followed by a violent thunderstorm and the whole sky suddenly grew dark.

The besiegers watched as the mighty walls crumbled under the onslaughts of the furious fire, the heavy rain and the gale, until all that was left were blackened beams and miserable piles of rubble. Vortigern had fallen; Aurelius Ambrosius was King.

Then, suddenly, the storm abated and the sun began to shine. From nowhere, Merlin appeared before the King. "I have come to advise you, Sire," he said earnestly. "You were right to first settle accounts with Vortigern, and you will know that you still have to fight the Saxons. The stars foretell your victory, but they also warn of your death if you should grant peace to your enemies. Keep this in mind and follow my advice!"

Before Aurelius Ambrosius could ask for an explanation, Merlin vanished into thin air.

So the Britons set about pursuing the Saxons and it was on Maisbel Field

that they caught up with them. There a decisive battle was fought in which the Saxons were routed.

The scene of the fighting turned red with blood. Most of the Saxons were slaughtered and only a handful managed to escape into the forests around York. Hengest, their leader, was taken prisoner.

It wrung the heart of Aurelius Ambrosius to see the battlefield, and the moans of the wounded nearly made him give the captured Hengest his freedom. However, he remembered Merlin's words and he ordered Hengest's head to be cut off.

Acting on Merlin's advice, the King had at first intended to have the remaining Saxons caught as well. However, when he heard that only a few were left and that they were living like wild animals in the forests, he left them in peace and devoted his attention to more important matters.

The long fighting had inflicted deep scars on the island. The fields had been laid to waste; the men-at-arms had burnt down many castles and settlements; people were starving.

The King did his best to make the country flourish once again. He installed a just order in the running of all affairs of state and the realm; he had the ruined churches restored. London was chosen for his royal residence, and it was here that the greatest amount of work was done at his behest, for he ordered not only new dwellings to be

built but also a magnificent cathedral.

Thus, Aurelius soon forgot about the danger that Merlin had predicted in such a mysterious manner. . . . .

Among the Saxons there lived a man called Eopa and he was the only one who understood the language of the Britons. He spoke it so well that he could not be distinguished from a native Briton. Thus, he did not even have to hide. Eventually, Eopa heard that the King had fallen ill, and he immediately moved into action. He shaved his chin and his scalp, dressed as a monk and, armed with many medicaments, went to see him. Certainly, at the time, a physician was what Aurelius Ambrosius needed most.

Eopa eyed him carefully and said, "Sire, you will be as sound as a bell again in a day or two. All you need is a restful sleep. I shall prepare a herbal brew that will make you fall asleep."

Thereupon the Saxon picked not only sleeping herbs but a deadly poison as well. He handed the potion to the King, and when he fell asleep, Eopa slipped out of the chamber unobserved. Aurelius Ambrosius never awoke again . . .

While this was all happening, Uther, the King's brother was, on Merlin's advice, pursuing the Saxons in the forests around York.

That night, after Aurelius's murder, a strange star rose over Britain. Its dazzling light seemed to cover the whole sky, but that was not all: the silver rays suddenly formed the likeness of a dragon, and from its mouth issued a flame which stretched from the land of the Gauls as far as the Irish Sea.

Uther just could not take his eyes from the incredible spectacle. But then Merlin, speaking in a soft voice, delivered another remarkable prophecy:

. . . Britain has lost its ruler, my lord, and since it is your star that has flared up in the heavens in the shape of a dragon, the time has come for you to take up the reign. And there is one more thing I shall reveal to you. The flame issuing from the dragon's head is a token of your son. His glory will surpass all the monarchs that Britain has ever known, and his empire will be among the most powerful in the world . . .

In such a way Uther learned of the death of his brother, that he had become king, and of the coming glory of his son.

Uther's was a prudent and just reign. He was known as Uther Pendragon — Uther Dragon's Head — since in memory of that heavenly sign he had adopted a dragon in his coat of arms.

The new King knew how to subdue the nobles in his realm and he made them obey all his orders and decrees.

The Duke of Tintagel was the only nobleman who took no notice of what the King said. Pendragon knew full well that he could humble the arrogant nobleman by force of arms, but he had no wish to start a new war.

Instead, he invited the Cornish duke and others of the nobility to a banquet in London, where they could discuss the whole affair together in a spirit of goodwill. To leave no one in doubt as to his peaceful intentions, the King invited not only the nobles but their wives as well.

So at Easter that year, one could see on all roads leading to London many horsemen in costly armour, as well as fair ladies in carriages laden with gifts. The great lords came from all over the island at the King's invitation.

The Duke of Tintagel was among the first to arrive and his wife, the fair Igraine, charmed all those at the banquet with her beauty.

However, it seems to have been the King himself whom she impressed most of all. From the very first moment he saw her, Uther Pendragon's eyes dwelt on her alone. As if he had entirely forgotten that it was the Duke whom he had in fact invited, he kept addressing Igraine. He poured wine

28

into her golden goblet with his own hand, and his eyes never had enough of contemplating her charming face.

He seemed to have become oblivious of the whole world and not even to hear the Duke when he asked if the King was willing to make peace with him.

That was what made the lord from Cornwall most exasperated. He hastily called his retinue, led Igraine out of the banqueting hall, and left London without bidding farewell to anyone. Only then did the King wake from his enchantment, and he decided he

would punish the rebellious nobleman, though, to tell the truth, what he most wanted was to see Igraine again as soon as possible.

Meanwhile, the Duke hastened to Cornwall. "The King will certainly not forgive me for this affront," he mused on the way, "and Tintagel is the only place where I can protect my wife. . ."

When he reached his castle, he had the moat filled with water, the drawbridge pulled up and all the gates firmly closed. But he did not stay there himself; with his faithful few he hid in a small castle nearby, called Terrabil.

Before long Uther Pendragon appeared at the walls of Tintagel Castle with a great army. At once he ordered the catapults, the battering rams and burning pitch to be made ready for laying siege. When he was about to give his order to start the assault he hesitated, and instead called for Merlin to appear before him.

"I don't know if what I am doing is right," he confided in Merlin. "The fact is that I want to see Igraine more than I want to humble the Duke, and it would be my death if she should come to any harm in the fighting that is before us. So give me your advice, since the future is no mystery to you."

This time Merlin answered only after a long reflection, "Sire, your heart beats only for Igraine, and I know what to do to make her become yours. But I will give you my advice only on condition that you comply with my wish. . ."

"I will do whatever you advise, just go ahead and speak," the King interrupted impatiently.

Merlin thought for a while and then he continued:

. . . Well, know then that the Duke is not here at all. You will find him a few miles away, in a small stone castle called Terrabil. So, it will not advance your purpose if you lay siege to Tintagel. Send your troops to Terrabil and I will help you get to your chosen one this very night.

It is laid down that Igraine will become your wife and will bear you a son called Arthur. But you will never see him, because I wish to take him away to bring up myself. That is my wish, Sire . . .

To Merlin's surprise Pendragon raised no objections. Such was his love for the Lady Igraine that he promised to do what Merlin asked of him.

Merlin, too, kept his promise. At dusk he gave the King a magic potion which altered his appearance and his apparel so that he could not be distinguished from the real Duke. By this subterfuge Uther Pendragon entered the Castle of Tintagel, where he was able to stay until morning, since Igraine believed him to be her husband.

In the meantime, the real Duke had thought up a plan to take the enemy by surprise and at midnight he and his men had broken out of Terrabil, fully armed.

But the besiegers had been on their guard. It was enough for the opening gate to creak, and a deadly rain of arrows had descended upon the Cornish troops. When the royal army had entered the small castle, no lives had been spared in a terrible slaughter and the Duke had been among the first to fall. Dawn broke at last, and it was Pendragon's banner that fluttered from the tower, announcing his victory far and wide. The King had no choice.

The moment he saw the banner he confessed everything to Igraine. And at that moment, as if to confirm his words, Merlin's potion ceased working and his own likeness was restored.

At first, Igraine bewailed the Duke's death and bitterly reproached the King for deceiving her. However, time healed her vexation; she made her peace with Pendragon and, when she realized that his love for her was enduring, a quiet and unostentatious wedding was celebrated.

Soon afterwards a son, who would be known as Arthur, was born to the royal couple. But before the happy father had a chance to see the boy's face, Merlin took the child and, acting on his promise, carried him away to an unknown place. . . .

TALE FOUR...
THE SWORD
IN THE STONE...

Arthur in Wales. How the Saxons try again to conquer the country, and Pendragon wins a glorious victory. The King dies. A new King — Merlin's prophecy. The sword in the stone. New Year's tournaments; the arrival of Sir Ector and Sir Kay with the young Arthur. Unwittingly, Arthur proves he is the true-born King.

Having taken Arthur from his royal parents, Merlin mounted his horse and headed north-west. His destination was Wales where Sir Ector, a good friend of Pendragon's, had his seat and dominion. It was to him that the wise counsellor was taking the boy — to be brought up along with Kay, Sir Ector's son.

Kay was several years older than Arthur. He had always wanted a little brother, and from the moment he saw Arthur, he scarcely budged an inch from him, and treated him with true brotherly affection.

Sir Ector, too, became fond of Arthur; after a time he regarded Arthur as his own son . . .

Thus the prince spent his childhood and boyhood days in Wales and that beautiful land of green hills became his home.

33

Then, Uther Pendragon fell ill with an incurable disease. For weeks and months he lay helpless in his bed; the doctors' efforts were unavailing, and even Merlin was at a loss as to what to do to help.

The tidings of the King's illness spread throughout the country. The nobles and the humble folk were sorry for Pendragon, but in the North, in Scotland, the Britons' perennial enemy, the Saxons, reappeared. With large armies, they marched for London in the belief that now the King was sick they could at last become masters of the island realm.

To begin with, their warring schemes worked. Whenever they were about to confront Pendragon's army, they would run away into the woods or hide on their ships near the shore. However, no sooner had danger passed, than they would reappear, burning, robbing, and capturing the defenceless.

In the end, with everyone fleeing from them in terror, the Saxons reached as far south as St Albans, hardly twenty miles from London.

At that time Merlin came to see the sick King and said in a grave voice, "The Saxons stand within a stone's

throw from here, Sire, and without you in command no one can stop them!"

"I would gladly mount my steed, but you can see for yourself — I can hardly move," said Pendragon.

But Merlin insisted. He gave the King a tonic, helped him put on his golden armour and his crested helmet, and before long Uther Pendragon stood at the head of his army at St Albans. As in the old times he firmly held his sword, and the dragon standard fluttered in the breeze.

When the Saxons saw the familiar horseman in golden armour they were seized with fear. They threw away their arms and took flight. But, with a strong voice, the King summoned his army to attack.

What a glorious victory it was! As if the dying leader wished to remind everyone of his warrior skill, he flung himself all alone into the enemy's ranks. With each dreadful stroke his sword turned red, and so did his golden armour, until the Saxons believed that they were being torn to pieces by an enraged red dragon . . .

With great glory and rejoicing Pendragon was carried to London on a litter, but while people throughout the whole of Britain rejoiced at the victory over the Saxons, the brave King breathed his last three days after the battle.

The land was cast into deep mourning. Igraine mourned the King most of all, and but for Merlin she might have died of grief. As it was, the wise counsellor consoled her with kind words and gave her to understand that before long she would experience an extraordinary joy that would make her forget her sadness.

After the death of Uther Pendragon, unrest began to spread in the land. "Who will become King now?" asked noblemen and common people, and many of the nobles wished to take the crown for themselves.

The confusion and turmoil grew, so that at last Merlin went to seek the Archbishop of Canterbury.

The Archbishop was a man of great faith, much esteemed by everyone, and nobody, even at a time of near-anarchy, dared to oppose him. He gave Merlin a kindly welcome because he knew that the counsellor was no less concerned about the fate of the kingdom than he himself.

And he was not mistaken; Merlin had come to ask the Archbishop to call all the noble lords together at Christmas and to tell them that the one displaying the greatest strength would become King.

The Archbishop shook his head in astonishment — a king need not necessarily be a strong man, he argued. He is to surpass the others rather in judgment and good sense, and to reign for the common good. However, when Merlin, in all secrecy, told the Archbishop the reasons for his request, he did not take long to decide and invited the nobility to come to London at Christmas-time.

Although a great deal of snow had fallen before Christmas that year and there were snowdrifts upon the roads, the barons, dukes, earls, and also poor freemen who had the right to bear arms, came flocking into London from all over the country. Every man was driven on by the desire to become King . . .

On Christmas Eve they all attended the morning Mass celebrated in the great London cathedral by the Archbishop himself, in honour of the future sovereign. They came out into the frosty air, and saw a wonder to surpass all wonders.

In the churchyard, in a place near the high altar, stood a great square slab of marble. In the stone was set a steel anvil into which a huge sword was driven. Letters of gold set in the stone read thus:

WHO SO PULLETH OUT THIS SWORD FROM THIS STONE AND ANVIL, IS THE TRUE-BORN KING OF ALL ENGLAND.

At once every man tried to pull the sword from the anvil. But none could move it a hair's breadth, though many of the knights were truly strong men and some tried their luck more than once.

The spectacle attracted some of the common people, too, who gathered

together in the churchyard and looked on with laughter as they watched the lords toiling with the sword in vain.

Eventually the Archbishop realized that the future King was not among the knights present. Therefore, acting on Merlin's advice, he announced that there would be tournaments and joustings on New Year's Day, thinking that the right man was yet to arrive.

Once again the snowbound roads leading to London became crowded.

This time, however, the visitors were attracted by the prospect of the games — to test their skills in wielding the spear, the lance or the battle-axe before the eyes of noble ladies and maidens. In those days, a triumph in such a contest was desired by everyone who bore arms.

Sir Ector, his son Kay and the youthful Arthur had ridden well over a hundred miles, all the way from Wales, to take part in the tournament.

To be exact, it was Sir Kay who was to participate. He had been made a knight not many months before and was just burning to prove his prowess.

Arthur was only getting on for fifteen and, according to custom, he acted as Kay's squire. He took care of his armour, and carried his lance and shield for him.

After a hard and tiring journey to London, they arrived on New Year's Eve and the three took lodgings in an inn near the city walls, not far from the plain where the tournaments and joustings were to take place.

Young Sir Kay could hardly sleep. No sooner had the dawn broken than he was clad in armour, which shone with being so new. He urged Arthur and his father Sir Ector to hurry for fear that he might miss something.

They arrived on the plain in good time and were overwhelmed by the crowds of people and the whole brightly-coloured spectacle. Suddenly, however, Sir Kay realized that, in his hurry, he had left his sword behind at the inn, and so he sent Arthur back to fetch it.

The young squire rode back as quickly as he could, but found the gate and all the shutters closed — the domestics themselves had been in a hurry to go and watch the tournament.

"What now?" Arthur wondered. His dear brother could not be left without a sword! And then he remembered that, when riding past the abbey, he had seen, in the churchyard, a sword set in an anvil.

So again he spurred on his little horse. The churchyard was quite deserted, and without thinking he slid from the saddle, seized the sword by the hilt, and drew it out as if it had been set into butter.

He did not even stop to read the golden inscription on the stone; quickly he remounted his horse and hastened back to Sir Kay.

"I have a sword for you, dear brother!" he cried from afar. But when he halted and saw the expression of surprise on Sir Kay's face, Arthur explained, "I know this is not your sword, but the inn was shut. This one may also serve your purpose; I pulled it out of the anvil in front of the abbey."

But Kay was not listening. He had taken a good look at the sword and the inscription the previous day, and he knew what it meant when someone managed to pull it out. He dashed off to Sir Ector and, holding the weapon before him, he blurted out, "I am King of England, father. This sword has decided my destiny!"

"And did you draw it out of the anvil yourself?" asked Sir Ector, shaking his grey head in doubt.

The young knight was rather taken aback. "Arthur brought it to me. But it was I who ordered him to fetch the sword. And anyway it would hardly be possible for a squire to become King," he said.

"We must make sure," said Sir Ector, as he made for the abbey in the company of Arthur and Kay.

Reaching the strange anvil, he halted and said to his son, "Now try to confirm your right with a deed, and drive the sword into the steel."

Sir Kay swung his arm with all his strength, but the weapon just clanged against the anvil and jumped off. Then it was Arthur's turn. With no effort at all, he drove the sword into the steel up to the hilt . . .

"Now you must pull it out!" Kay gripped the weapon again, but no matter how hard he tried he could not move the sword an inch. Arthur then tried again and easily drew it out and drove it into the anvil several times in succession. It was clear that only Arthur could be the true-born King, and both Sir Ector and Kay fell on their knees before the young man and kissed his hand.

"Rise, father and you too, my brother! Why do you bow your heads before me?" exclaimed the young man in surprise.

Sir Ector explained:

. . . Because you and no other are the true-born King if this land. You are not my real son and you are not Kay's brother, even though I brought you up as such. The truth is, you were brought to me shortly after your birth by the wise Merlin; your real father was Uther Pendragon and your mother was the lovely Igraine.

The fact that you managed to draw the sword from the anvil proves your right. None other than the true King could succeed in this . . .

With these words, Sir Ector rose and led the astonished Arthur to the Archbishop to tell him of Arthur's glorious deed.

However, few of the lords would believe what the young man had accomplished and, over a period of time, Arthur was obliged to pull the sword out of the anvil three more times before their eyes, the last time being at Whitsun.

By then, even the most envious persons and the worst doubters with their objections and sneers about Arthur being too young, had to eat humble pie. Most of the nobles, and the common people as well, wished Arthur the joy of the crown.

Thus, the Archbishop blessed the King's sword and the most celebrated of the warriors dubbed the young man knight.

Not long after, Arthur would be crowned!

TALE FIVE . . .
KING ARTHUR'S
FIRST VICTORY . . .

Arthur's coronation. Departure for Camelot. Preparations for the festivities and the siege of the castle by the armies of the six Kings. Arthur's first victory. The terrible battle in the Bedegraine Forest, and how Merlin puts an end to it. Arthur's return to Camelot and why Morgan le Fay and his three nephews come to see him.

Like the sun that gilded that memorable coronation day with its rays, so the youthful King shone among all the nobles and knights of celebrated name. And there, at his coronation, Arthur swore the oath both to the lords and the commoners that he would be a kind and just ruler to them all until his dying day.

He then listened to charges about the slights and injustices, mostly perpetrated by the rich and powerful nobles upon the weaker ones after the death of King Pendragon. Acting on the advice of the wise Merlin, he passed immediate judgement, punishing the offenders and compensating their victims. In appreciation, the majority of those assembled acclaimed Arthur, but some of them — and those were among the most powerful — started grumbling about a beardless boy taking such liberties . . .

Next, Arthur appointed the royal dignitaries. Sir Kay was nominated Lord Seneschal, Sir Ulfius became Lord Chamberlain, while Sir Brastias as Vice-Regent was charged with the defence of the realm in the north, for it was from the north that an enemy invasion threatened, whether by Scots, Picts or Saxons.

As the sun was about to set, the young King announced that he would proceed to Camelot Castle the next day, where he would hold a great banquet with jousting to celebrate his coronation.

Camelot was a very strong stone castle, now thought by some to have been near to Winchester. Merlin had suggested that Arthur should make it his royal seat and that he should go there with his retinue as soon as possible. So, even before the wisps of

the morning mist had descended upon the Thames, Arthur's banner, sporting its red dragon, was streaming in the wind far outside the city.

No sooner had they reached Camelot than Sir Kay commanded all Masters of Hounds to secure enough partridges, pheasants, hares, boars-meat, venison and fish for the banquet. Sir Lucas, the Lord Butler, was charged with looking after the drinks, and particularly to see that there was plenty of claret. Others were ordered to put up wooden barriers around the

field where the jousting was to take place, and to build scaffolding and pavilions for the distinguished guests.

What a commotion there was all around! The huntsmen, carpenters, cooks, servants — in fact everyone in the castle's domestic service — were busy as never before. In the large field under the castle, beyond the jousting place, tents began to spring up like mushrooms for the arriving noble guests and their men-at-arms who had come to attend the celebration.

Their numbers grew into hundreds,

44

even thousands. Apart from barons, dukes, yeomen and mere freemen, there were six kings, each of them with an unexpectedly large number of knights. King Lot of the Orkneys, King Uriens of Gore, the King of the Scots and King Nentres of Garlot were present, as were King Carados and the King with the Hundred Knights.

Arthur was delighted with so many distinguished guests, but Merlin contemplated the teeming bustle under the castle, gloomily.

"Are you not pleased to see so many lords come to pay me homage?" asked the young Arthur. The counsellor ran his fingers through his greying beard before he replied, "There is no need for me to foretell the future to answer you, Sire. Just look at that field. So many men-at-arms do not as a rule accompany a nobleman to a festival or a tournament. And their tents? They should be made of bright-coloured taffeta, not of canvas so they look like a war expedition! . . ."

"So you think they want to do battle with me?" Arthur considered, and when Merlin nodded, he resolved, "I shall send them precious gifts, as should a host and king; only then shall I see . . ."

Although Merlin objected on the grounds that bestowing favours on an enemy is entirely pointless, Arthur insisted and sent gifts to all the six Kings.

But he was soon to find out his mis-take. Instead of offering thanks, they sent word that they would not accept anything from such a milksop, still less allow him to rule them. They would present him with their own gifts by the blows of their swords and spears — and then it would be decided to whom the crown did belong!

The news made Arthur's blood almost boil, and at that moment he would have been ready to rush out all alone, sword in hand, against the overbearing Kings. But Merlin soon calmed him, and advised him to stay in the Castle with his faithful followers for the time being. He pointed out that some of those outside were sure to join Arthur and his men, many of the knights having come to Camelot with entirely honourable intentions.

For two weeks Arthur's men remained in the Castle keep and during that time their numbers had actually doubled. The six Kings treacherously laid siege to Camelot with their armies, but all the others joined Arthur's side, so that the forces were almost equal.

After that Merlin no longer restrained the young King. He even helped him to put on his armour and girt him with a sword. Then Arthur ordered the Castle gate to be opened and he broke out on to the field at the head of his knights. Behind him at a gallop came Sir Kay, Sir Brastias and Sir Ulfius, but before they had time to join the fray, there was Arthur hacking at his astounded enemies with such might and main that many sought safety in headlong flight.

In fact, at that moment the armies of the six Kings were divided and so, while half was fleeing in disorder from the dragon banner, King Lot, the King with the Hundred Knights and King Carados, with their men-at-arms, were attacking Arthur from the rear.

But the fortunes of war did not favour them, either. No sooner had they overrun a few straggling men-at-arms than they had to face Arthur's knights who pressed and flayed them hard. The Castle garrison joined in with clubs and cudgels and before long the hostile Kings had no other alternative to a thorough thrashing, but to take to their heels.

Thus ended the first battle fought by the youthful King, and by his bravery, he gained his first victory.

He had really fought like a lion, so it was no wonder that the knights and barons had nothing but admiration for him, and Sir Ector went about saying, "It was as if I saw King Pendragon in the days of his glory; nay, the boy displayed even more courage!"

"There is no army in the world that could beat us now," maintained Sir Kay, but Merlin who had listened to much idle talk in silence, suddenly cut him short. "Do not be foolish enough to think that the six Kings will give in so easily. And you, Sire," he said turning to Arthur, "had better send for reinforcements. This was but a skirmish, the real battle is yet to be fought . . ."

Merlin's words of warning spoiled everybody's joy over the victory but, as always, they proved to be true. Before many days had passed, those dwelling at Camelot learnt that the six Kings had been joined by another five, and that those eleven Kings were already mustering a tremendous armed force in the north.

Arthur did not delay. He sent Sir Ulfius and Sir Brastias to France to seek aid from the brother kings, Ban and Bors, who had helped Uther Pendragon to wage his wars in days long past.

King Ban was staying a while in the city of Benwick. Today, some believe that the site of Benwick is Bayonne; others say it is Beaune. Ulfius and Brastias were pleased to find King Bors there as well, so they expressed Arthur's entreaty to the kings, together with the understanding that Arthur would come to their aid against King Claudas, their own powerful enemy.

Ban and Bors gave both knights a kind hearing and, after a brief counsel, they came to an agreement that they would cross the sea to England with one thousand knights at All Hallows.

Meanwhile, Arthur was gathering men-at-arms in England. About twenty thousand agreed to join him and, on Merlin's advice, he led them north, to the Bedegraine Forest, which in those

days covered the wide area between the Humber and the Trent.

Merlin, himself, waited for the armies of Kings Ban and Bors at Dover and, having met them, he set out with the reinforcements towards Bedegraine. However, the foreign troops did not join up with the royal army. Instead, Merlin hid them in the thickets so as to have them in reserve.

Towards the evening of that day, a mounted patrol reported that the armies of the eleven Kings were advancing from the north in such numbers as made men's hair stand on end in terror and it was said that the earth trembled under the weight of the ironclad men. The enemy army crossed the Humber and pitched camp at one end of the plain where King

Arthur had his encampment at the other end. The night before the battle seemed a very long one.

Dawn had hardly broken when the two armies opposed each other in deployed lines. Although the odds were so much in favour of the men-of-arms of the eleven Kings that their knights were three to one of Arthur's, they were not the first to attack. Sir Ulfius and Sir Brastias hoisted their standards and took the field, followed by three thousand men with swords and spears . . .

Like an iron wedge they penetrated deep into the enemy ranks with a terrific onslaught, dealing blows right and left. Brastias himself, in the confusion, unhorsed his adversaries so fast that they had no time to lift their shields in defence; Sir Ulfius found it hard to protect his right flank as agreed on, for he could not keep up with his friend's horse. Unspurred, the animal would ride into the fray and beat with its hoofs as if they were metal-sheathed clubs.

But then King Lot became aware of

49

the danger which threatened from Brastias and Ulfius and shouted to his knights, urging them to swoop on the two immediately. They cut them off from the others, stabbing and hacking their horses from behind until they fell to the ground.

But at that moment Arthur, Sir Kay and Sir Ector joined the battle with their forces. From the distance, the young King saw Brastias lying on the ground and Ulfius, on foot, defending him desperately with his broken sword. The sight gave his inexperienced arm a wondrous strength. He cut in two the first attacker's helmet and shield and, toppling a second into the dust, he tied the enemy's stallion to his own steed.

He did not notice that, King Lot,

sword drawn, was rushing at him. But Sir Kay did, and he stabbed Lot's outstretched arm so hard with his spear that a stream of blood spurted forth. Assisted by Arthur, he helped Ulfius to the saddle of the captured stallion, and then looked about for his father. The old knight was doing passing well! Maybe ten of the enemy were attacking him, but he covered himself so successfully with his shield that he did not sustain a single scratch. He also helped several enemy knights out of their saddles.

Then, it was none other than King Carados who had to flee from the battle in shame, and on his own two feet — for before he had time to recapture his own dapple-grey, Sir Brastias was astride the horse and riding off into the fray.

King Lot, seeing Arthur, for whose

honour the whole battle was being fought, among those fighting, re-grouped his army and rode against Arthur's men in great force. The attacked men fought like lions and every step of their retreat was soaked with the blood of the Northerners yet, thanks to their superiority in numbers, the enemy gained the field after a few hours.

Then, as the armies of the eleven Kings began to close in upon Arthur, the knights of King Ban and King Bors hurled themselves from the undergrowth like a whirlwind.

"Alas, we are lost!" cried King Lot, as he recognized King Bors of Gaul. "If we stay divided, nothing in the world will save us from those Frenchmen!"

And indeed, his fears were well founded. The two Kings did honour to their banners, entirely disregarding the odds against them. Under their blows, enemy helmets shattered like egg-shells; a single thrust of their spears was enough to pierce the breastplate and the coat of mail. Nor were their knights and foot soldiers any less strong and battle-tried.

When, an hour later, thousands of the enemy had fallen in the bloody battle, King Lot retreated across the stream, to re-form his men.

Now it was plain to see that Arthur had more men-at-arms. Perhaps no more than ten thousand exhausted men remained to fight on the side of the eleven Kings that late afternoon, and these knew full well that death was sure to be their lot. They could not even think of retreating — that would make them all the more easily a quarry. So they silently awaited their fate and King Lot, himself, was perhaps the quietest of all.

And it was at that moment that Merlin rode out on to the open space between the two armies. In the very middle he pulled up his tall black horse violently and cried out in a voice that rang on all sides. "Are you not in terror of death yet?" he called. "It is death who has gained the field and if you carry on, it is he and no one else that will triumph!"

Then he turned to the eleven Kings. "You must know that you have nothing to gain by this war," he said. "Well, leave the booty here as the vanquished should, and hasten to your homes. Your country has been attacked from the sea by the Saracens, and unless you stand up to them, you will soon be Kings without Kingdoms!"

Then Merlin said to Arthur, "Sire, the fortunes of war were on your side because you fought for a just cause. But be advised. Put a stop to the fighting lest death should prevail! There are still many battles awaiting you; let your first one not prove to be your last!"

And that was the end of the famous battle. The enemies hastened away leaving, according to custom, much excellent booty on the battlefield.

Arthur gave most of this to the brother kings, Ban and Bors, and rewarded his knights according to their bravery in the battle.

Then they returned to Camelot to celebrate the victory by a grand feast and to retell, over their wine, the story of the battle. Arthur invited the Kings Ban and Bors, Sir Ector, Sir Kay the Seneschal and some of his other gallant knights to his own chamber, wishing to bestow special favour and honour on these, his friends . . .

After the feasting they were sitting on furs talking as Lucas the Lord Butler filled their goblets. All of a sudden, a trumpet sounded from the Castle gate, announcing the arrival of guests. Looking out of the window, Arthur saw an entirely unknown lady standing at the gate, and she was accompanied by three young knights.

"I am Morgan le Fay, the King's sister," she declared to the guard and as if to confirm this, she ran towards Igraine, Arthur's mother and embraced her.

By then Arthur, too, had followed his mother down from the tower and he gave her a questioning look.

"Morgan really is your stepsister," said Igraine. "Her father was the Duke of Tintagel, and later she married King Lot of the Orkneys."

The moment Arthur heard the name of King Lot, his cheeks burnt with anger. However, before he had time to give vent to his rage, the oldest and the most stalwart of the three knights escorting Morgan stepped before him and addressed him. "We bring you news, Uncle," he said. "Our father has allied himself with King Ryons of North Wales and together they have besieged King Leodegrans at Cameliard. If you go to Leodegrans' aid, we shall be happy to join you . . ."

Arthur had often heard Merlin talk about King Leodegrans and how they, together with Uther Pendragon, had fought the Saxons and become true friends. So he answered at once, "We shall take the field tomorrow. But why aren't you on your father's side? Why do you wish to join me, against him?"

"Because we know he is not in the right when he is fighting you," said the young knight. And then added, "And also because you are our uncle."

And so in the end Arthur, satisfied, asked the three young knights their names. Those names were Gawain, Gaheris and Agravain.

TALE SIX . . .
EXCALIBUR . . .

An expedition to help the King of Cameliard. Arthur duels with a strange knight, Sir Pellinore, on the shore of an unknown lake, and is saved by Merlin. Excalibur, the gift of the Lady of the Lake. The battle of Cameliard. King Lot is killed by Sir Pellinore. Arthur is enchanted by Guinevere. Merlin disappears.

When the Castle gate was opened the next morning and many knights in full armour rode out, the armies of Ban and Bors did not head westward to Cameliard to help Arthur. Instead, they rode straight in the direction of Dover.

Indeed, the previous night, tidings arrived that King Claudas was cruelly laying waste the lands of the two brothers and that the garrisons of their castles would be hard put to hold out unless quick help was forthcoming. Thus, both Ban and Bors had to bid Arthur farewell, so as to sail home without delay.

The young King expressed regret at not being able to join their expedition, but Merlin persuaded him to set out for Cameliard. "Leodegrans is in great danger and, if his castle falls, it will open the way for the enemy's advance.

55

Do not forget how strongly King Lot wants revenge!"

For six whole days they journeyed, and during all that time more and more knights joined the royal army. Arthur did not ride at its head this time, but handed over the command to Sir Kay and, with Merlin at his side, he rode along the byroads and bypaths.

Eventually, he arrived at an unknown lake. On the shore was a multi-coloured tent. Driven by curiosity, Arthur spurred his horse to draw closer but, suddenly, a huge knight on a mighty horse came rushing at him, his visor lowered and his lance couched against his thigh. "Whoever wants to ride past the lake must first fight with me!" cried the knight.

Arthur called back, without fear, "Gladly! But you can see yourself that all I have is my sword!"

Instead of replying, the knight shouted something into the tent, and out ran a squire, bringing long lances for the King.

Then, without further ado, the two opponents rode against each other with their weapons at the ready. The clash of their lances was deafening, but they both remained in the saddle. However, the lances had not stood the impact and the metal fragments flew to the four winds.

Arthur was on the point of drawing his sword, but the knight stopped him. "Now it is for the spears to have their say, isn't it?" he asked.

So two blunted spears were brought from the tent, and once again the adversaries spurred their horses and charged. This time, however, Arthur's weapon slid off the iron armour, while the unknown knight struck a mighty blow right into the middle of the King's shield.

In an instant both Arthur and his horse tumbled down to the ground, but he was swiftly on his feet with his

sword drawn. "Dismount and show how you can use the weapon most honourable for a man!" he said angrily.

At once the giant of a knight dismounted from his horse, seized his weapon and cried, "I shall be honoured to fight a man who does not give in easily. But this time it will be a life and death contest!" And with those words he pounced, like a boar, on Arthur.

In the fight, sparks flew from the swords and the armour of both men soon became stained with blood, but neither would yield. They fell to the ground and rose again, until at last they tangled so violently that Arthur's sword broke in two, like a dry twig.

The knight immediately felled the King to the grass, and then raised his sword saying, "You are in my power, and unless you acknowledge yourself beaten, you shall die!"

"Rather death than a shameful mercy!" cried the powerless Arthur and the giant's weapon swished through the air. But it did not land. The unknown knight fell as one dead, and someone raised the King from the ground.

It was Merlin! He was smiling but Arthur was seething with anger. "Leave me alone, I would rather perish in an honourable fight than see you deprive that good warrior of his life by your spells!" he cried.

"Do not be sad, Sire," said Merlin placatingly. "All I did was to make a deep sleep descend on him. When he wakes, he will come to you of his own free will and put himself at your service. . ."

"What then is his name?" asked Arthur.

"Pellinore of Wales. Do remember that name, for one day his son, Percival, will extend the renown of your court," replied Merlin mysteriously. Then he added, "Now let us hasten to catch up with the men-at-arms, Sire, they are all waiting for you, impatiently."

"But with such a sword I shall hardly be of any help," said Arthur mockingly, pointing at the broken blade.

"That is easily remedied, my lord," said the counsellor lowering his voice. "Look at the lake!"

Arthur was amazed to see the surface of the lake ripple and waves spread from the middle, although there was a dead calm. Suddenly, a slender arm clothed in snow-white samite emerged from the water, bearing a shining sword.

"It is yours, Sire. Go and fetch it!" Merlin whispered.

By a stroke of luck there was a barge hidden in the reeds. Arthur climbed into it and found the oars. He rowed to the middle of the lake and, when he took the sword, the arm immediately vanished. The next moment, the King saw a maiden of heavenly beauty, clad in white, walking with graceful steps over the water. She smiled at him and then descended into the deep.

When Arthur had steered the barge to the shore, he was so excited that he could not utter a word. So his faithful counsellor explained, "That was the Lady of the Lake and mistress of all waters. The sword she has given to you is called Excalibur and it will bring you many victories."

"Indeed, it is beautiful," the King sighed, examining with admiration the golden blade and the hilt set with precious stones.

"It is a weapon of more value than ten others," Merlin spoke again. "As long as you have it upon you, you will lose no blood in the fights to come. If you lose it, you will lose your life. Mind that you never forget this, Sire!" he warned.

When Arthur and Merlin returned to the royal army, they were joyfully welcomed by one and all. Sir Kay addressed Arthur. "It is high time, dear brother, for me to hand back the command to you. They say King Ryons and King Lot are already laying siege to Leodegrans' castle with a force of ten thousand knights."

Arthur just nodded saying nothing. Then he spurred his horse to a quicker pace and in a few moments his horsemen and foot soldiers were rushing down the vale after him, like an avalanche. When the countryside again opened out before them, they saw in the distance that Sir Kay had been right. There were ladders set against the walls of Leodegrans' castle, and in many places the enemy had broken into the courtyard. Fires and a black pitchy smoke showed that the attackers were trying to set fire to the tower.

"Quickly; be quick!" commanded Arthur and, sword in hand, he dashed down the slope. Out of the corner of his eye he glimpsed the few knights who kept pace with him. They were Sir Kay, Sir Gawain and, on his powerful horse, the now familiar knight from the lake — Sir Pellinore!

The castle gate had already been thrown off its hinges and so, like a tornado, they rode into the rearguard of the astounded besiegers. Before they were aware of the attack, the enemy was cut down like sheaves.

Arthur forced his way alone as far as the tower, where the enemy ranks were the thickest. Under the blows from the magic Excalibur, shields and helmets burst and startled horses threw their masters into the dust. The defenders, at the tower windows, just watched in amazement.

Nor was Sir Pellinore any less successful. Not far from the tower he saw the standard of King Lot and, crying out, he charged. He pierced Lot's horse with his spear, and before the ruler of Orkney had time to raise his shield in defence, Sir Pellinore hacked at his neck until the King's head flew off.

This was the sight that met the eyes of Sir Gawain, King Lot's son, and the horror of it shocked him senseless. He let go of his horse's reins, and Gringolet — such was his horse's name — wisely carried him to a secluded spot away from the roars of battle.

The enemy soldiers, too, were seized with terror and confusion. They saw the broken standard of the ruler of Orkney; they saw his senseless body; and they saw that Arthur's ever increasing reinforcements were rushing in. So, King Ryons gave the order to retreat. He drove his horse against the wall to make the stallion jump it at the spot where it was lowest. Driven by despair he succeeded, and escaped, but most of those who tried to follow him did not. Their horses tumbled into the moat, neighing with pain, and many a knight broke his neck in trying to jump that wall.

At that moment King Arthur stopped the fighting — for there was but a handful of the enemy left, and these were thinking of nothing but fleeing to save their lives.

The battle had been won. The old King Leodegrans held Arthur in his arms and with tears in his eyes praised his valour.

However, there was yet another who came to pay tribute to the victor. This was Guinevere, King Leodegrans' daughter. The whole time the battle had raged she had watched Arthur from the turret window, fearing for his life and later, when he entered the castle, she helped him remove his

helmet and armour and she dressed his wounds and bruises.

As for the young King, he could not take his eyes off the charming maiden. He wanted to stroke the shining bronze hair which reached down to her waist and to look into her deep blue eyes. Perhaps that was why he seemed struck dumb in the damsel's presence. Eventually, Sir Kay and Merlin led him away to the banqueting table that Leodegrans had spread with meats and drinks in his honour.

On the return journey to Camelot, Arthur was like one daydreaming, and it was only after reaching the Castle that he roused himself from his enchantment.

It was Merlin's advice that Arthur should organize a glorious funeral for his fallen enemy King Lot, as behoved a high-born knight.

A magnificent tombstone was hewn and guests were invited, including

King Lot's widow — Arthur's sister — Morgan le Fay, and her three sons. They arrived in deep mourning. Then Merlin lit twelve long wax-candles upon the tombstone and, as they were all slowly leaving the cemetery, he joined Arthur and whispered to him, "From now on, Sire, I shall be more often on my travels than at Camelot. If you wish to know whether I am safe and well, just look at those candles. As long as they burn, there is no need to fear. If they go out, have people search for me. . ."

With these words Merlin left Arthur. He mounted his bay, and rode off without disclosing to anybody where he was going. For months and months there was no news of him, but the candles on the tombstone burned with a clear light. However, there were some knights-errant who rumoured he had been seen with the Lady of the Lake.

TALE SEVEN . . .
SIR BALIN . . .

A damsel from the Isle of Avalon visits Camelot and is delivered of her noble sword. What adventures with that sword befall a poor knight named Balin. How he takes King Ryons prisoner and triumphs over an invisible enemy. Sir Balin's sad death.

The great battle was over, and days of peace descended upon Camelot Castle. Merlin's candles were burning with a calm and steady flame; no new enemies appeared and the most stubborn of them, King Ryons, seemed to have been swallowed up by the earth.

Thus Arthur was able to dedicate himself to his duties as King, but he also had time to find pleasure in royal revels. Among his favourite pursuits were hunting and knightly joustings. Before long these made his Court so famous that the finest tournament contestants from all parts of the country and from overseas came upon their steeds to meet at Camelot.

It was just after one of these celebrated tournaments, when both victors and vanquished were sitting in harmony in the Castle banqueting hall repeatedly going over all the contests and even the individual blows, that the door flew open. Before anyone knew

63

what had happened, who should be
standing in the middle of the hall but
a tall damsel veiled from top to toe in
a pleated cloak of purple. The radiance
of her golden hair flooded the huge
room with light.

Silence fell upon the hall; all present
were holding their breaths when the
damsel said, "I have come from the
island of the dead, the Isle of Avalon. . ."

"And how can we oblige you, fair
maid?" It was King Arthur himself
who at last broke the silence.

"It is little that I ask of you," she
replied. "Since the best knights of the

land are present at this Court today, one of them may not find it difficult to deliver me of this sword. . ." And she let the mantle fall from her shoulders. All could see that she was girt with a sword, whose beautiful inlaid hilt marked it as the work of a craftsman of excellence.

All the knights, eager to help a lady in distress, rushed towards her. But the sword was so fast in its sheath that no one, not even King Arthur, could move it, even by an inch.

One by one, they tried and then bowed their heads low. Soon there was only one knight remaining who had not tried to unsheathe the sword. His name was Balin and, by his humble attire, he seemed to be the poorest of the knights.

"Why do you not try, Sir?" asked the damsel, drawing nearer to his table.

The youth shrugged his shoulders. "It seems pointless to try my luck when warriors much more noble than I am did not succeed," he said. "But if you insist, then I will try."

Sir Balin rose, took the sword by the hilt, and to everyone's immense surprise, he drew it from its scabbard with the greatest of ease.

"Thank you, Sir Knight," smiled the beautiful stranger. "So I have not come to Camelot in vain after all. But now give me the sword again, I still have a long journey to go."

However, Balin shook his head.

"No, I am going to keep it, fair maid," he answered, "because I have earned it. Only he who overthrows me in battle can claim it."

The damsel's smile suddenly froze. "Do not forget that I come from Avalon! If you do not return the sword to me, it will destroy you. You will, within a short time, cause immense sorrow to others and the greatest grief to yourself that will send you to your grave," she warned.

"Do you mean to say that I shall pierce myself with the sword, or cut off my own head?" laughed the knight scornfully. "No, no, you can't fool me so easily!"

"I have warned you in good faith," said the damsel sadly. She wrapped herself in her pleated mantle, and was suddenly gone, leaving behind only a sweet fragrance.

When all at last had recovered from the strange happening, they saw that Sir Balin, too, was hastily preparing to depart.

"Many of you, and even you yourself, Sire, are looking outraged," said Balin. "But that sword is worth a life to me. I can't afford one like that. I shall use it only to fight your enemies, in order to deserve again the favour of you and your knights."

In vain, Arthur tried to detain Balin with kind words and to explain to him that his deed was not condemned by anybody, least of all by himself. All Arthur could do, was to make Balin

promise that he would come back to Camelot as soon as ever he could. And with this the poor knight left the Castle. . .

While Balin was guiding his horse's steps over hill and dale, another horseman was following him closely. This was Sir Lanceor, who was a son of the King of Ireland. He was perhaps even more desirous of gaining the damsel's sword than Balin himself, and so he was now getting ready to ambush him. He had had time enough to prepare a plan.

Balin was wearing only a simple jacket and hose thrust into ragged old boots, and save for the sword, his only protection was a leather shield. Lanceor rode behind him clad in full armour. He wore a plumed helmet and a metal shirt over his armour, with iron gloves and spurs. He could hardly be seen behind his huge shield. A sword in a scabbard swung at his girdle but, in addition, he wielded a spear in his hand.

As Sir Balin rode through an oak forest, lost in thought, the Irish knight spurred his horse and, catching up with Balin, he ordered, "Halt and surrender your weapon to me, if you wish to preserve your life!"

Balin brought his horse to a stop with a single pull of the rein, and turned to face his pursuer. "Not that easily, Sir Knight!" he answered. "Though I cannot see your face, you must first win the sword in an honest joust!"

"I am Lanceor and come from the green island of Erin. I wish to avenge the wrong you have done to the damsel of Avalon!" came the reply. Then the Irish knight couched his spear and made a fierce charge against Balin.

Balin just waited as if rooted to the ground. When the heavy blow from the spear pierced his leather shield, he averted its point by the sheer strength of his arm. Lanceor found himself on the ground and, before he was able to rise, Balin was above him. For the first time he used the new sword to strike an enemy. He slashed away without thought, suddenly seized with a savage and implacable fury. . .

After a while he realized that Sir Lanceor was dead. Suddenly, a rider bore down on him, along the forest path; he saw it was a woman on a palfrey. "Oh, what have you done, Sir Knight?" she cried. "Do you not know how much I have loved Sir Lanceor?"

Balin was about to reply but, as he opened his mouth, another bloody spectacle was enacted before his eyes. The damsel jumped from her mount, seized Sir Lanceor's sword and, with its hilt pressed against the ground, she threw herself on the point with the full weight of her beautiful body. Her senseless shape slipped down into the grass beside the dead Irish knight.

As though in a dream, Balin looked at the two lovers who had been so full of life only a few moments before. It began to dawn on him that the curse of the Maid of Avalon was being fulfilled.

"Really, you should not have kept that sword," a calming voice beside him said and, looking round, he saw Merlin. "The only thing you can do at the moment is to have the couple buried with appropriate honours," Merlin continued, "then we shall see."

And so they searched for a suitable place for the lovers' last rest, but did not find one. Eventually, they met Mark, King of Cornwall, and he helped them, by finding a magnificent crypt in a nearby church.

At that time King Mark was a kind and compassionate man, and he was favourably disposed towards the young lovers. Before long, however, as we are to learn shortly, he was to become a changed person. . .

However, let us return to Sir Balin. When the burial was over and the ruler

68

of Cornwall had bidden them farewell, Merlin said to the knight, "I do not know if this will alter your fate but, if you wish, I can advise you as to how you can regain your good name."

"Why should I not wish it? Indeed, this is the very thing I am anxious for more than anything else!" exclaimed Balin, catching Merlin by the hand.

"Well then, listen!" said the counsellor. "Not far from here is a secret path through the thicket along which King Ryons, with but a few men, rides once a month to see the Lady of Vance. On this path you can easily seize him, and bring him to Arthur as your prisoner. But take care you remember one thing — you must not kill Ryons!"

Balin swore an oath upon his new sword that under no circumstances would he kill Ryons. Then the sooth-sayer led him to the hiding place from which he was to ambush the king.

It was nearly midnight before Ryons and his armed men appeared. Just as they were passing the hiding place, Balin jumped out and began to deal blows with his sword at the cluster of men-at-arms trying to defend their king. One after another they fell, until Ryons remained all alone. Balin, entirely forgetful of his pledge, lifted his sword to strike. . .

"Hold back, you poor wretch!" Merlin's furious voice could be heard, and Balin froze like a statue.

Merlin pushed the terrified king clear of the sword and chided Balin severely. "I can see there is no changing your fate. Is it honourable to slaughter defenceless prisoners? No! I cannot talk to you any more. Now go and take Ryons to Camelot. Let at least King Arthur have a good opinion of you!"

Having said this, Merlin vanished into the night, leaving Balin and his noble captive to set out for Arthur's Castle.

This time King Arthur gave the poor knight a glorious reception, and he received his enemy with due honours. Thanks to Merlin's negotiating skills, he even made King Ryons pledge that, henceforth, he would never take the field against Camelot.

And once again the poor knight set forth from the Court, though this time they all tried to make him stay, most of all King Arthur himself. However, the knight was restless and he hastened to meet his inevitable fate.

He rode through beautiful countryside as well as through wilderness, encountering many adventures until, upon one road, he met a horseman who was behaving in a very peculiar way. Though he was of a mighty, even giant stature, and though he carried a sword at his girdle, one that Balin would have found hard even to lift, he was forever turning round fearfully in the saddle — his head swivelling like a weather-cock. When he came nearer, he cowered and clung to the neck of his black steed with such vigour that his black beard all but merged with the horse's mane.

"Why are you behaving in such a strange way, Sir Knight?" asked Balin, unable to hold back his curiosity. "Is it perhaps because you suffer from the falling sickness?"

The horseman smiled sadly. "I am waiting for death," he replied, "but I do not know from which side he is going to strike. I am being pursued by an enemy who has the power of invisibility, and his weapon may cut short my life at any moment."

"That is a treachery I will not stand for!" cried Sir Balin.

"And what can you do to prevent it?" asked the strange knight.

"I shall personally take you to Camelot, you will be safe there!" said Balin.

The two set off together, but their ride did not last long. No sooner had the knight told Balin that his name was Harleus the Bearded and that his invisible enemy was called Garlon, than a long spear came flying from the depths of the forest. It pierced Harleus's chest and, as Balin stood over the dying man, he was entreated, "Do not leave my death unavenged. Do not let Garlon cause further misfortune . . ."

After burying Harleus, Balin rode on. He met more and more victims of Garlon's treachery and he followed the horrible trail for a long time without finding Garlon. Then he stopped for the night with an old nobleman, who told him, "I know where you can find the invisible knight. This villain has dishonourably killed my own son." Then he continued, "Not far from here is the castle of King Pellam, and there you will find Garlon, for he is Pellam's brother. There you can see Garlon's real face and meet him in equal combat. But do not forget that King Pellam is an expert at jousting. You will hardly overcome both of them!"

Balin kept silent. He just took with him the stump of the spear with which Garlon killed the nobleman's son, and set out for the castle.

It was not long before the castle gate opened in front of him. At first the knight was puzzled, but then he learnt that on that very day King Pellam was holding a great banquet to which he had invited nobles from far and wide, both known and unknown. So, Balin got into the banqueting hall without difficulty, although he did have to wait a while before receiving permission to retain his sword.

There was lively commotion at the

banqueting table. As usual it was the fair maids and ladies who drew the greatest attention, but many a man also attracted the eye, whether for his magnificent attire, his remarkable face, or his conduct.

"Who is that dark-faced knight who sits next to King Pellam?" Balin asked the neighbour on his left.

"Oh, don't you know Sir Garlon, our sovereign's brother?" said the man in surprise. By then, however, Balin, crazed with anger, had stepped towards the royal table. "You are a capital pair of brothers, to be sure!" he called across the room. And when he at last took his stand in front of Garlon, he raised his voice even more for everyone in the hall to hear. "It is easy for you, sir, to win when the opponent does not know from where he is to expect the death-blow. And you, King Pellam, look on complacently while such foul deeds are done."

"I do not know what you are talking about, but I will not take such insults!" said Garlon, reaching for his sword.

But Balin was faster. "About this!" he cried, and before anyone could move to stop him, he struck Garlon a blow direct to the heart with the stump of the knight's own spear.

That was how the life of the invisible knight came to its end, yet it was not the end of the fighting for Balin. King Pellam now jumped to his feet and charged the knight, sword in hand. However, Balin's weapon had

come from the legendary Isle of Avalon. Their swords clashed only a few times when the king writhed in pain and blood upon the paved floor. Then, to everyone's amazement Balin the Savage, as he had been nicknamed, began to tend the wound which he had inflicted.

No man in the banqueting hall challenged him and King Pellam himself, having partially recovered, paid tribute to his fighting skill. "There are few among the knights of my acquaintance who are your equal in swordplay. But remember, it is not merely the sword that can help you to win," he said.

"What else then?" asked Balin.

"The shield!" laughed the king and went on, "I am well aware that you show contempt for the shield to prove your courage. However, only a proper shield can protect you from a treacherous arrow or spear."

Balin agreed. "You are certainly right," he said. "But I am still so poor that I cannot afford such a shield. . ."

"Before we part and you leave my castle, I am going to select one for you myself," interrupted the king.

And that settled the matter. Balin rode off in quest of further adventures armed with an immense shield and left his small, leather shield at King Pellam's castle. . . .

His reputation preceded him and few dared to oppose him. He was feasted and worshipped everywhere, and when he took part in tourna-ments, his hosts considered themselves honoured, because he was always victorious.

One day, however, he did meet his match. A certain knight's castle stood on a small island in the middle of a wide river and, leading his horse to the ford, Balin could not help noticing an inscription in golden letters mounted on a mighty oak:

'Whoever dares approach my castle without permission, shall be punished by my own hand!'

"Oho!" laughed Balin on seeing the sign. "I wonder who can stop me!" He remounted his horse and without hesitation spurred him into the water.

He had not even reached the middle of the stream when a horseman in flaming red armour rushed from the castle into the river. Without a shout of warning, he lowered his spear and stormed towards Balin.

Balin, just in time, managed to lift the huge shield bearing King Pellam's coat-of-arms, and the attacking spear broke into splinters. But the knight in the flaming armour charged again. This time he raised a heavy sword with both hands. Again Balin used the shield to ward off the terrific blow, but his steed fell from under him, the blade having nearly separated the horse's head from its body.

Balin rose heavily from the shallow water, expecting to be dealt his death-blow. But curiously enough his opponent drove off his own white horse, and so the odds were again equal.

Blow after blow rained from either side; the rivets in the armour burst and both knights bled until the river ran red. Yet still they remained on their feet.

Then Balin's adversary dropped both his weapon and his shield and fell into the water. And, at that moment, Sir Balin, wounded to the death, saw his face and recognized him as Balan, his own brother.

"You alone were able to overthrow me," whispered Balan, his strength ebbing.

Step by step, and each supporting the other, they tried to reach the river bank, yet step by step also life was leaving their bodies. And it left them completely the moment they reached the grass. . .

It was there, too, that Merlin found them, held in each other's arms. And again it was Merlin who had them buried in one tomb over which shone the inscription:

'Here lie Balin and Balan,
brothers who perished
by each other's sword
without either of them knowing
the other.'

TALE EIGHT...
THE MARRIAGE
OF ARTHUR
AND GUINEVERE...

Arthur's wooing of Guinevere and how Merlin and King Leodegrans agree on their marriage. The royal wedding in London and the journey to Camelot. The Knights of the Round Table. The Siege Perilous, and Merlin's prophecy. The wedding feast.

When Arthur was getting on for twenty years old, the lords began to urge him, good-naturedly, to bring himself a bride to Camelot. This would, as they said, increase his royal renown. They even started inviting to the Castle charming princesses and high-born maidens. The young king became annoyed at this and preferred to roam the forests with his hunting retinue. Fortunately, Merlin appeared at the Court at this time, and so Arthur had somebody to open his heart to.

Merlin listened carefully to the King's complaints and then he asked, "And you yourself, can't you think of some maiden you would wish to make your wife?"

"I know of one such maiden," Arthur confessed after a while, blushing a little. "She is Guinevere, daughter of King Leodegrans of Cameliard..."

Whereupon Merlin frowned and asked, "And indeed, can't you think of

any others? I know even lovelier damsels who would make much better wives."

"You seem to understand everything better than I do," Arthur interrupted him angrily. "Take notice, however, that I shall never choose another as long as I live!"

Merlin only shrugged his shoulders and with a friendly smile said, "Well, it cannot be helped. If a man's heart is set, it cannot be changed. I only know

that in the distant future, when my bones are rotting in the grave, a terrible war will break out among friends because of Guinevere."

Not even Merlin's gloomy prediction could persuade the King to give up his chosen bride. "He is getting old, the wise man, and who knows if he has not been too much influenced by the Lady of the Lake, as people say," thought Arthur to himself.

In the days that followed, Merlin no

78

longer mentioned his doubts in front of the King; on the contrary — he, himself, chose presents from the workshops of the best goldsmiths for the bride and for her father, and he, himself, nominated the wooing party and rode at the head of the magnificent procession to Cameliard.

The wooing party reached Cameliard safely, and Merlin conveyed Arthur's wishes to King Leodegrans. The King said with a smile, "This is the second time your master has done me a great honour. I wish for the marriage with all my heart, if only to honour the memory of Uther Pendragon, my greatest friend. But we shall have to speak to Guinevere, also."

Who should enter the hall at that moment but the damsel herself. Therefore Merlin, using flowery language, told her of Arthur's wish and then, speaking for the wooing party, he added, "We bow before you with confidence in our hearts, for we trust that the beauty which has no equal in the land, is in you allied to virtue and nobleness of spirit."

All the while Guinevere kept silent; a blush suffused her face under the flood of her shining hair. Then, having heard what Merlin had to say, she said with a quiet voice, "Happy shall I be to become Arthur's Queen. For never have I heard of a warrior of greater valour, nor of a more powerful King."

After this, the damsel smiled happily, and went to her chamber. Presently, they could hear her singing.

"After all, she is only sixteen," said Leodegrans to Merlin in excuse, "and can hardly conceal the joy that has come to her so unexpectedly. I am afraid it will be left to us to settle everything about the marriage."

And this they did. It was agreed that the glorious event, together with the Queen's coronation, would take place in London before Christmas, while the wedding feast would be held immediately afterwards at Camelot.

There was not much time left after the wooing party's return for all the preparations. There was the banqueting hall to decorate, the feast to make ready, and the noble guests to invite.

As for Guinevere, she, like every other bride, was all in a flurry about her wedding dress. Every maid-servant was made to go through every piece of brocade, velvet, silk and ermine with her, so that the future Queen could make her choice.

In the end, however, everything was ready and at the appointed hour the wedding guests rode in procession to the Cathedral. Never before had London seen such a magnificent sight. Spectators, in numbers untold, gathered there from far and wide, and made a truly merry time of it.

Leading the procession were jugglers, acrobats, musicians and jesters, all parading their skills. Many a clownish person played pranks on those standing around, so that the music, singing and shouting mingled with merry laughter.

Then the bride appeared and a hush of admiration fell over one and all. It is hard to tell whether it was the splendour of Guinevere's hair, the loveliness of her face, the gems in her tiara, or the snow-white ermine, that took everyone's breath away. In low whispers they pointed out to one another the large jewel which glittered from the pommel of Guinevere's saddle. This was believed to drive away foul diseases and to illuminate the night.

Before long Arthur himself came riding into view amidst mighty cheering and rejoicing, for even the simplest

The people waited patiently in the close and, as the bells rang in jubilation, the King stepped out to distribute gifts to the assembled crowd. Whole handfuls of gold and silver coins were scattered in the close by Arthur, while King Leodegrans and Sir Ector equally honoured the old custom.

And thus the glorious ceremony came to an end and the wedding guests set out for Camelot. And what a merry procession it was. The peasants had strewn green twigs and

of peasants paid tribute to the King's valour and sense of justice.

His suite was made up of Sir Ector, King Leodegrans and Sir Kay, all in their festive robes. Only Merlin was dressed plainly in his usual grey cloak, as ever grave and severe.

However, who would pay much attention to the counsellor, when here was a chance to set eyes on Arthur's famous knights, fair ladies and damsels in their dozens, even hundreds!

They entered the Cathedral and the doors were shut. The Archbishop joined Arthur and Guinevere in holy matrimony. After the Mass, several young noblemen, Gawain included, were dubbed knight by the King.

branches along the entire route, and in every fort and village through which they passed, the King was welcomed with joy and acclamation.

Yet even this was as nothing compared with Camelot. There the Castle, and in particular the banqueting hall, was decorated with brightly-coloured silk draperies. Arthur had had exotic flowers brought in from southern climes, and Merlin used his magic powers to preserve them as if newly picked.

The guests never ceased to wonder at those miracles, and when Arthur had offered gifts to each, according to his degree, they pledged him their knightly faith and aid in good times and bad.

Then King Leodegrans rose and said, "I too have brought a wedding present for you, my son. Its value may be expressed by the very virtues which have been shown here."

At Leodegrans' command, an enormous Round Table, with one hundred and fifty seats known as sieges, all beautifully carved, was brought into the hall.

"This is the Round Table," went on the old King. "At one time it was to have served your father and his warriors, but Uther Pendragon never lived to see peace and calm in the land. So I give it to you with one hundred fine knights who will render you faithful service unto death, until your dying day. All the sieges are the same, so that no one may exalt himself above any other; neither is there to be any difference between those who sit around it like a band of brothers."

King Leodegrans fell silent and Merlin then spoke. "Therefore be seated at the Table, all of you who wish to be faithful companions and knights to our King, though it may cost you your lives." Then, turning to Arthur, he continued, "And to you, my Sovereign, I say these words: it is in this Table that your power and glory resides. Therefore, do not let its sieges ever become entirely empty!"

The knights then took their places at the Round Table. In addition to those brought by King Leodegrans, there were Arthur's warriors, including Sir Kay, Sir Ector, Sir Pellinore the Strong, Sir Ulfius, Sir Brastias, Sir Lucas and Sir Gawain. No sooner were all seated, than each knight's name, written in letters of gold, appeared on his siege.

Some of the sieges, however, remained empty, and about these Merlin went on to prophecy, "In years to come, these will belong to heroes whose adventures the whole world shall know. This, however, is the 'Siege Perilous' destined for the saintliest Knight of the Round Table," and he pointed to one of the vacant seats. "Yet it shall be many years before that knight comes along. Therefore let none of you sit at that siege, lest it should cause him to perish."

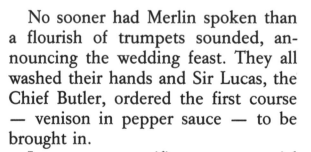

No sooner had Merlin spoken than a flourish of trumpets sounded, announcing the wedding feast. They all washed their hands and Sir Lucas, the Chief Butler, ordered the first course — venison in pepper sauce — to be brought in.

It was a magnificent ceremonial feast, the like of which is hard for us to imagine today. The venison was followed by stuffed partridge, then came wild boar, pheasant and chicken prepared according to various recipes, hare and waterfowl, and then pastries of every possible sort.

The guests all ate slowly and with restraint. Even so, after a few hours, many could eat no more. Only Pellinore, the giant, his hands and beard dripping with fat, was still hard at it, as if to bear out the truth of the saying that a valiant knight is given to good eating, which keeps him from ever becoming a coward.

Then, a pie as big as a cart wheel was brought in, and the young Queen herself set about carving it with great care. Everybody started up in fright and amazement when small birds of all kinds came flying out and set their course toward the windows and out to freedom . . . Yet not even this meant that the feasting had ended. For, when the guests had moistened their throats with claret, it was a sign for various kinds of fish to be brought in (Sir Pellinore had a particularly enjoyable platterful of eels) together with cheese, cakes, fruit and choice nuts.

Long into the night the guests remained banqueting at the Round Table, and for their entertainment there were musicians playing, bards singing, and jugglers performing their incredible feats.

However, at a certain hour, King Arthur and his bride bade them goodnight, and took themselves to their consecrated bed. Again, the deft fingers of the musicians made the strings ring out and the words of songs went echoing into the night . . .

TALE NINE...
SIR GAWAIN AND THE GREEN KNIGHT...

More about the wedding revels. A strange green guest tries the strength of the Round Table Knights. How Sir Gawain cuts off the Green Knight's head, and how the head challenges him to a duel in a year's time. Sir Mordred and Beaumains arrive at Camelot. Sir Gawain's quest for the Green Knight and his adventure with the lady of the castle. How the quest ends, and the lesson learned about women's wiles.

In celebration of Arthur's wedding, the feasting and merrymaking continued at Camelot till New Year's Day. Outside there was a heavy fall of snow. It settled in silent snowdrifts, but every now and then the wind raised it into eddies, and every little crevice had the blizzard wailing in it.

However, in the hall where mysterious shadows and lights from the fire flickered, there was singing and telling of tales, and Queen Guinevere, like a lovely rose that beautifies a garden, lent glamour to the company.

When all had received their New Year's gifts and the knights once again fell to telling of their adventures, the King suddenly grew pensive. "I would much rather experience such adventures," he thought to himself, "than

just listen to them being recounted."

Suddenly, the great door flew open with a crash and a clang letting in the snowstorm, and into the hall rode a strange man upon a huge horse.

He was so tall and strong that none of the knights was his equal. Even Sir Pellinore, the strong man, looked tiny beside him. But the strangest thing about the knight was that his hair and thick beard fell down his back and chest like spring grass, and were of the same bright green colour. Under his cloak of green fur he wore, around his waist, a green belt set with amethysts, and his hand clasped an axe with a flashing green edge. The stranger's horse looked like a fairy-tale steed. There were snowflakes melting on its green mane and the water ran over its mossy neck and down to its gold hoofs. The horse's green saddle and its trappings were richly inlaid with gold.

"Who is the governor of this castle and these men?" he asked in his great booming voice.

A moment of deep silence fell upon the company. The Green Knight gave a searching look at each man in turn until the King rose from his seat and said, "Let me bid you welcome to the Round Table, Sir Knight. You have come just in time to join us in our rejoicing — in the celebration of my marriage to Queen Guinevere."

"So you are King Arthur, are you?" answered the Green Knight, as if unable to believe his ears. "And the other beardless youngsters are the redoubtable Knights of the Round Table, I suppose? Well, I must test your valour."

"None of us is going to do battle," the King stopped him with indignation. "Surely you too must know that Yuletide is the season of peace and quiet joy."

But the Green Knight only laughed aloud in mockery. "Who is talking of doing battle? For have I not left my helmet, sword and shield at home? However, when no one cares even to test his valour, I can see that I am dealing with a band of cowards!"

At this Sir Gawain, the youngest of the Knights, sprang up. "We have had enough of your insults," he cried. "I take the challenge myself—so be quick and name your conditions."

Again the Green Knight only smiled as though unaware that the young man was about to draw his sword. Then he said, "It is something of a game. You will strike me one blow with this axe as hard as you can, and exactly a twelve-month from now I shall return the blow."

A murmur of wonderment shot through the hall. Only Sir Gawain spoke. "Where shall I find you?"

"It will be a long trek; you will have to find the Green Chapel. But now, come and strike," the Green Knight urged Sir Gawain, handing him his battle-axe. Then he knelt down and, having bared his neck, he laid his head upon the Table as if upon the block.

Sir Gawain showed no hesitation. He gripped the green handle with both hands, swung the axe, and sent the Green Knight's head rolling across the floor like a cabbage.

"It is something of a game!" Sir Kay's voice aped that of the green guest. The others looked on, horrified.

But the Green Knight neither faltered nor fell. He rose from the table, took the severed head into his arms and, as if nothing had happened, he sprang on the back of his waiting horse.

And it was the head that then spoke. "Mind you do not forget, Sir Gawain; exactly a twelve-month hence there is the return blow awaiting you at the Green Chapel!" it said. And with that, the strange visitor rode out into the blizzard.

So, the New Year's adventure ended. After a while, all again made merry. Sir Gawain alone stood staring at the wall, where hung the green axe left behind for him by the Green Knight . . .

Then longer grew the day, and frost and snow
In the hills subsided when March dame in.
Fresher looked the lea, and springs rippled;
Now the green bank reflects in water blue.
Again the sweet scent of violets, resins; the singing nests
Or mysterious pools do entice you.

But onward!
Speed, knight, to the plot
Where shimmers summer's air.
Ride forth towards adventure
Till you come to Camelot . . .

That summer, many came riding to Arthur's Court, not a few of them desirous of serving the King faithfully, and becoming his regular companions at the Round Table. One who came was a knight with a foxy face, called Mordred, who declared that he, too, was a son of King Lot of Orkney.

Although warned by Merlin he should keep out of Mordred's way, since through him the whole Round Table was fated to perish, Arthur allowed him to remain at Camelot.

Mordred was too much given to flattery to win people's affection, unlike the young lad who accompanied him and found his way to everybody's heart.

The lad was a simple rosy-cheeked young fellow and, when asked by Arthur about his name and his wishes, he answered, "Sire, I have three wishes.

For one year I wish to be near you, and will do your bidding in all things. I shall need only food and a place to sleep. Later, I will let you know my other two wishes, and then, even my name."

"You may do as you please," smiled the King and sent for the Seneschal Sir Kay, charging him to take care of the lad.

As it happened, Sir Kay was the only one who did not like the young man. "He must be a shepherd's son rather than a son of King Lot, when all he cares for is food and somewhere to sleep," he muttered under his breath and, without further ado, he had the boy helping in the kitchen. Nor was he slow in finding a name for him. He mocked the lad by calling him 'Beaumains', thus making fun of his big and still rather clumsy hands.

The name caught on, but Beaumains did not mind in the least. He did his best in the kitchen and kept his thoughts to himself . . .

Then days grow shorter, clouds are heavy with rain,
With yesterday's flame but a woeful shadow now.
Of grey mists does Autumn weave its thread.
Again the weeping of leaves, now shed like a robe
Roams through the vale, again night shall come
With no full moon or stars; the time of departed souls.
And the Castle?
A solitary keep does rear
Its head in late October
And parting time is near.
Hear, Gringolet is neighing . . .

In the meantime, Sir Gawain had not forgotten the pledge given to the Green Knight, and it was just after Halloween that he set forth in search of him. At Camelot everyone was sad to say goodbye to Sir Gawain, and they had little hope of ever seeing him alive again.

Of course, it was Sir Gawain himself who felt the most sick at heart. But he plucked up courage and donned his finest armour. He took his sword and his shield with its pentangle device, a five-pointed star which protected him from all evil. Then he mounted Gringolet, his war-horse, and like an arrow, shot out through the Castle gate.

For days and weeks he rode north, through marsh and mire, fording many a river and stream and roaming among woods and rocks. But in vain did he ask for the whereabouts of the Green Chapel.

A heavy snowstorm closed upon him one day and deeper and deeper Gringolet dropped into the snowdrifts, his rider tormented by the cold. Yet Sir Gawain pursued his quest till he came into the desolate wild land of North Wales where, in a deep oak forest, he realized that it was Christmas Eve.

For a long time he had not set eyes on a living soul—and he nearly despaired of ever leaving the forest. At last, however, he found himself in open parkland, and Gringolet stopped on a wide snow-covered plain. The Knight saw a mighty castle set on a hill in front of him. Following a path, he arrived safely at the great gate and, after his first call, the porter lowered the drawbridge to let him in.

He was immediately surrounded by squires and serving men who helped him to alight. Before long the lord of the castle and his wife came to meet him, he strong and broad of shoulder and she enchantingly fair—never in his life had Sir Gawain beheld a lady more fair. Both bade him welcome with equal sincerity and joy.

"Welcome, wherever you have come from! Be my guest for as long as it pleases you to remain in this castle,"

said the nobleman. But Sir Gawain only answered with a sigh that he must soon journey on, so as to be at the Green Chapel on New Year's Day.

"Indeed, it is but a few miles from here, so why all the haste?" came the reply. This was good news to hear, and Sir Gawain readily agreed to stay at the castle until New Year's Day.

He spent the festive season in good cheer and merriment. His host and hostess bestowed all care upon him, and equally kind were the knights and ladies being entertained at the castle.

The day before New Year's Eve, the lord of the castle was sitting with Gawain in the hall, and after a brief conversation he said to him, "I shall be hunting deer tomorrow, and it would be a pleasure to invite you also. But I believe you will be better advised to save your strength for the Green Chapel." Then he went on, "However, I promise to give you the best that I may win in the forest. All I want in return is whatever may come to you, here in the castle." Sir Gawain thought this a really strange proposal, for what could possibly come his way here in the castle? However, he agreed.

Next morning, at daybreak, the courtyard rang with the excited voices of the huntsmen, the snorting of impatient horses, and the baying of the hounds. Every huntsman had a last check of his bow and quiver full of arrows. Then a fanfare of horns was sounded, the castle gate was flung open, and the hounds and horsemen set forth into the gloom of the forest.

The chase was on. The startled game ran out of brushwood, arrows whizzed through the air, and the hounds rushed along the blood-stained track. The sun was rising. The snow glittered under the hoofs of the horses panting with exertion; but the band rode on, with their hearts pounding.

Sir Gawain was still asleep at the time. Only when the door of his chamber creaked, did he awake. He was astonished to find the fair lady of the castle coming towards his bed.

"You must be a very sound sleeper, Sir Knight," she said with a smile. "Instead, you should be serving me since we are left here alone together."

"With pleasure, fair lady. For it will indeed be my greatest joy to serve you in all things," Sir Gawain replied, somewhat puzzled.

"You really wish to become my knight?" she asked.

"Thus do I pledge as a Knight of the Round Table," answered Sir Gawain.

"Now, you must confirm your pledge," smiled the lady, and she leaned towards him, catching him unawares with a kiss. Before he had recovered from his amazement, she had left the chamber and was gone.

All through the morning Sir Gawain escorted her wherever she went and with every moment she seemed to him more beautiful. Yet she did not say a word about the morning kiss.

After lunch, when the maids had cleared the table, she suddenly said, "In faith, you have really served me like the best of knights; here is my reward." And again she gave Sir Gawain a kiss, this time so long and sweet that he felt an enchanting mist envelop his senses. However, before he recovered, the lovely lady was again gone and he did not see her appear again during the whole afternoon.

At dusk the moon appeared in the sky, and Sir Gawain was expecting his host to return from the hunt.

Instead, he heard the lightest of footsteps, and the enticing lady again stood before him. She laid her arms on his shoulders and asked, "Could you ever serve another lady as her knight?"

"No, not even Guinevere," Sir Gawain answered, his heart throbbing. "Were it not that you are already wed, there is no other I would desire to be my wife."

At that, the lady kissed him for a third time. Then she unwound from her waist a length of green lace and handed it to him.

"That is what I too would desire," she said. "Therefore take this magic lace to remember me by. It will protect you from every blow, Sir Knight, but tell no one of this gift."

Soon after, Gawain's host came home from the hunt, and having put away his bows and arrows, he ordered the servants to bring in the game he had shot.

"As agreed, I give my best spoils to you," he said to Sir Gawain, pointing to a fine hind laid on the floor. "This one I got in the morning."

Sir Gawain said nothing, but reached across and gave him a kiss. The host acted as if he had not noticed it, and ordered that the next trophy be brought in. It was the head of a stout wild boar. "I shot him after midday, and it was not an easy job either," he said.

And again, Sir Gawain rewarded him with a kiss.

Finally, the pelt of a fox appeared, and this time the lord of the castle received three kisses in return.

He then inquired of Sir Gawain how he came to possess such gifts, but he received no answer, nor did he learn anything about the gift of the green lace . . .

On New Year's Day, a blinding blizzard raged when our hero rose and got ready for his quest for the Green Knight. Sir Gawain wore at his waist the length of green lace. The squires helped him to buckle on his armour, and brought out Gringolet for him to mount. The lord of the castle explained to him the way, and the knight said goodbye to him and his wife.

Among hollow rocks he had to guide his steed with the snow blinding his eyes, but Gringolet rode on safely until they reached the stream upon which his host had said the Green Chapel stood. Yet there was nothing like a chapel to be seen; only a murky cave yawned on the opposite bank.

"A very devil's oratory it is, rather than a holy tabernacle," thought the Knight, as Gringolet forded the stream.

But no sooner were they on the other bank than a rumbling of falling stones could be heard. A mighty figure of a man clad in green armour and wielding an axe in his right hand, stepped out from the hollow.

"It is good that you have kept your word," the Green Knight welcomed Sir Gawain.

"Every Knight of the Round Table is in honour bound to keep his vow," answered Sir Gawain. "But let us not tarry," he said, glancing at the shining axe, and then he took off his helmet, baring his neck for the stroke.

His adversary stepped forward towards him, and swung the deadly weapon. Try as he might, Sir Gawain could not avoid flinching at the sound of it.

"Ha, do not tell me you are a coward! I never flinched from your blow, though my head fell off!" mocked the Green Knight.

Thereupon Sir Gawain bent his head again, and this time he stirred not an inch. The axe whizzed through the air biting into his neck and drawing blood. The blood stained the snow, but the wound was not at all deep.

And that moment Sir Gawain noticed that his adversary was making ready to strike again. "No, this is beyond our bargain!" he cried. "Only one blow was agreed on a year ago."

"That was a year ago," answered the Green Knight, "and it is you who have not kept your bargain—the vow which you gave me but yesterday." And with that he lifted his green visor, revealing the stern face of the lord of the castle. "Yes, only yesterday, since not everything you received in the castle has been given to me," he cried.

Sir Gawain blushed with shame, and started undoing the girdle of green lace. But the Green Knight restrained him. "Keep it, dear friend, as a warning against women's wiles," he said. "For it was with my knowledge that my wife beguiled you. And remember that many excellent wise men and warriors, like Solomon, David and Samson, fell victim to such—whereas you are still a beardless youth."

There was nothing for Sir Gawain to do but to accept this well-meant advice, though one question still disturbed his peace of mind. "Tell me at least who you are, and how you come to know such incredible magic," he asked.

The Green Knight smiled. "I am Sir Bercilak, the Knight of the Lake," he said. "And I learnt my magic from a damsel who beguiled Merlin into teaching her. She sent me to Camelot to test the valour of King Arthur and his Knights . . . But now get on your way, the King must be worrying about what has happened to you."

So Sir Gawain rode Gringolet through the snowstorm as fast as he could to Camelot, to tell everyone how he had fared in his quest for the Green Knight.

TALE TEN . . .
SIR CYNON,
SIR UWAINE,
AND THE LORD OF
THE FOUNTAIN . . .

The strange adventure of Sir Cynon at the castle of the twenty-four maidens and his lost duel with the Lord of the Fountain. Sir Uwaine experiences an even stranger adventure in the same place, the outcome of which is a surprise not only for himself but also for the Knights of the Round Table.

For a long time the Court at Camelot discussed the Green Knight and the beauty and deception of his wife, and it must be said that Queen Guinevere and all her ladies-in-waiting greatly enjoyed the gossip. However, other stories were being told as well, since Camelot Castle stood wide open to everybody. Many who had originally intended to pass by the Castle, were pleased to call in, and some became members of the brotherhood of the Round Table.

One of these was the young Sir Uwaine, son of King Urience of Gore. As we know, the King had, until recently, made war on Arthur. Sir Uwaine, however, took no heed of his father's earlier hatred and became earnestly devoted to Arthur and his companions. Little wonder then that he championed the cause of the Queen and her suite.

This gave rise to the following adventure.

One day a knight named Cynon called at Camelot Castle and, according to custom, he was asked to recount something remarkable that he had experienced.

"Well, there is not much to tell, for I am sure to be the youngest among you here," the young man began, and his glance swept from the face of Sir Kay the Seneschal to those of the strong Knight Pellinore, Sir Gawain and others. "But here is my story.

. . . One day upon a sudden impulse I had my horse saddled and rode out aimlessly over hill and dale to seek adventure. I do not even know how long I rode, whether for a single day or

a week, but then a hardly noticeable path led my horse into a beautiful dale. Birds were singing everywhere and I saw a boar and several small herds of hinds or roe-deer. Salmon were springing up over the rapids of the stream winding through the valley.

Then in the most beautiful spot over one creek I saw a castle towering on a rocky headland. Its towers were so slim that Camelot looks like a fisherman's cottage by comparison . . .

"How dare you affront the royal . . ." started Sir Uwaine, jumping up from his siege and about to draw his sword. But Arthur restrained him and Sir Cynon went on:

. . . Nor is that all, of course. In a small field bellow the castle I saw two lads learning to bend the bow, and the bows were of pure ivory. Their coach was an elderly gentleman, perhaps their guardian for all I know. And all three were arrayed in brocade which was so gold-embroidered that it dazzled the eyes. Believe it or not, should they appear in this hall everyone would feel like a beggar . . .

"How dare you!" the hot-blooded Sir Uwaine cut Cynon short again. But, once more, Arthur calmed him down, and the story continued:

. . . Then the guardian led me to the castle and there I saw twenty-four maidens, all weaving that same magnificent brocade. I could not take my eyes from their faces, so lovely they all were. I dare say that not even the beauty of our Queen Guinevere would outshine theirs . . .

"How now? What did you dare to say?" Sir Uwaine was up on his feet again, backed this time by an agreeing protest from all the ladies present.
"Just leave him alone and let him finish the story, though he cannot be said to excel in politeness," said the Queen, looking up from her embroidery, and smiling. Sir Uwaine sat down again, disgruntled.
Sir Cynon, as if unaware of the commotion he had caused, went on undisturbed:

. . . And at once they gave me every attention. Some looked after my horse, others divested me of my armour and weapons which they at once began to clean, others then dressed me in that same golden brocade, and six of the maidens brought in meats and drinks, the like of which I had never tasted in my life.
In the course of the meal, the elder-

ly man who had been training the lads in the meadow — and he must have been the king himself — suddenly said to me, "I know full well, Sir Cynon, that you left home in quest of an adventure. So I trust you are content, here."

Truth to tell, I had never until then seen such wonders as those at that castle in the dale, but my restless

blood drove me on. I explained this to my host and he said,

"In my young days my wish would have been the same, but I must warn you beforehand — you will have only yourself to blame if any misfortune befalls you."

On the morrow, at early dawn, I bade farewell to the kind king, the lovely maidens and the lofty castle, and rode on through the dale. But the journey was no longer so pleasant, let alone as comfortable as before. The forest became more and more impassable, my horse stumbled its way over rocks, and the little stream which until then had been my guide became lost in the undergrowth. Nevertheless I had no thought of turning back.

Then at last a little more light appeared among the stems and branches; my horse quickened his pace until we found ourselves in a large glade. In the middle, upon a little knoll, I saw another wonder. Sitting there was a real ogre, one-eyed and one-legged, and most terrifying of all was the horrible bludgeon in his hand which he began to swing in a menacing manner the moment he spotted me.

I evaded him as best I could, until the hulking big fellow got tired and said quite peaceably, "What on earth are you seeking in these parts, you human worm? Who has sent you here?"

"The king of the twenty-four maidens sent me, for I am seeking adventure," I answered truthfully.

At that the one-eyed creature looked me up and down, from head to foot, and broke into a loud laugh. "Such a milksop?" he mocked. "I think you should still be carrying a lady's train. Why don't you learn horse-riding or the use of arms rather than ride out into the world like this? However, so be it. You are the architect of your own fortune . . . Less than an hour's ride from here you will see a tall fir in a small glade. Underneath it there is a fountain surrounded by marble, to which a pitcher is tied with a golden chain. Fill the pitcher with water from the fountain and pour it over the marble slab. Believe me, at that moment you will experience such an adventure as you have never dreamed of in your life!"

I spurred my horse on and before long I could see the fir, which was so tall that its top seemed to touch the sky. And beneath the fir was a glittering fountain circled with marble as white as snow.

I dismounted to fill the pitcher and, acting on the advice of the one-eyed ogre, I poured the water over the slab. But this I should not have done! For no sooner had the water begun to trickle down the stone than I heard the clatter of hooves in the distance as if a storm were coming. A horseman appeared at the gallop. He was all in black and his lance, held for the attack, was tipped with gold, dazzling to the eyes.

Hardly had I managed to remount and lift my shield in defence than he dealt me such a terrific blow to the shoulder that I fell, and rolled in the dust under my horse. I feared that my shoulder, together with my arm, had been separated from my body! The Black Knight circled around me but, when he saw my plight, he made me a mocking bow and, in a moment, was gone. The hooves of his black horse once again reminded me of thunder which, fortunately, was now receding!

Well, that is the end of my most amazing adventure, I must thank Providence that the end was not more disastrous! . . .

Cynon's adventure gave rise to a long discussion. Everybody joined in, except Sir Uwaine, who sat like one dazed. Then, taking a very early leave of the whole company, he went to bed.

However, early next morning, when Camelot was till hidden in the mists, Sir Uwaine was seen, in full armour, leaving from the gate. Cynon's words had greatly disturbed him and he had decided to go, himself, and face the Black Knight of the fountain.

It is not known for how long Sir Uwaine searched for the lovely dale with the castle of the twenty-four maidens, or when he finally saw the one-legged, one-eyed ogre and, at last, reached the fountain. But, at least, unlike the youthful Cynon, he was more than well prepared to duel with the Black Knight.

When the thundering clatter of the hooves sounded in the distance, and the dark enemy rushed in like a whirlwind, Arthur's warrior did not wait for him to strike the first blow. Unexpectedly, he reined over his horse, and then smote his attacker in the side with his sword. The black horse's momentum carried the Black Knight on. He circled the whole glade, then, at a slow trot, he began to ride back to the castle.

Sir Uwaine followed the black horse from a distance. His enemy was leaving a bloody trail behind him, and it was obvious that he was growing weaker and weaker.

Then suddenly the city walls were before them. With a rattling of chains the drawbridge was lowered, and with a clank and a clatter the protective guard in the gate was lifted.

The Black Knight rode through the gate, and Sir Uwaine spurred his horse to follow. But the Black Knight had disappeared among the houses of that unknown city and Sir Uwaine found himself in an empty street, not knowing which way to turn.

Then he saw the trail of blood. This led up the hill to where the towers of a castle were visible. Suddenly Sir

Uwaine's path was crossed by a maiden wearing a long white mantle. "Do not ride further, or it will be your death!" she cried and, catching his horse by the rein, she pulled him into a narrow side street. He was led through a hidden garden-gate and into a closet with a small, narrow window. Here she explained her actions. "The Black Knight, here called the Lord of the Fountain, is mortally wounded, and the whole castle is up in arms to put paid to the man who has inflicted such a wound on him. But I know that you are one of the Knights of the Round Table, and that it was an entirely honourable fight. So I shall hide you in this closet until danger has passed."

"You are kind to me, fair maid, and I do not even know your name," said Sir Uwaine courteously.

The maiden replied, "My name is Lynette, and I am one of the ladies-in-waiting of the Lady of the Fountain, who is the wife of the Black Knight..." Her words were interrupted by loud cries and the wailing of women, coming from somewhere inside the castle, and then the castle chapel bell started to toll. Lynette frowned, then turned and left the chamber.

When, a little later, she reappeared, she was wearing a black mourning robe. "Our lord has died," she explained. "The mourning cortège is now on its way to the chapel."

Sir Uwaine looked through the small window. He could see the figures in their black robes and they were led by a tall lady whose hair shone like fire against her black clothes, while the loveliness of her face was enhanced by its paleness.

"Who is she?" asked the Knight, unable to tear his eyes away from such sad beauty.

"She is the Lady of the Fountain whose husband you have slain," replied Lynette.

She was amazed to hear Sir Uwaine declare, "No one else but that lady do I wish to have as my wife. You must help me, or there is no purpose to this life that you have saved."

In vain, Lynette tried to warn the knight against appearing before the Lady of the Fountain. She would have preferred to keep Uwaine's love for herself and she was also aware that his life was still in danger. However, at Sir Uwaine's insistence, she sought out her mistress.

Lynette heard her cries and lamenta-

tions as she wondered who, after her husband's death, would successfully defend the Fountain and the whole realm. She gently suggested that her mistress should turn to King Arthur's Court, where she would be sure to find a new protector as well as her new lord.

The Lady of the Fountain was angry. "Do you, the one I have loved best, advise me to do that?" she cried. "Do you want me to trample underfoot the memory of the Black Knight so soon after his death? Get out of my sight, before I set the hounds on you!"

With tears in her eyes, Lynette returned to Sir Uwaine in the secret closet.

The next day, however, the widow summoned Lynette to see her, and said, "I could not sleep because of your words. Now, I realise that what you said was meant to be helpful."

While Lynette bent her head so her mistress could not see the relief on her face, the Lady went on, "We really do need a brave knight and a fighter. As you said yourself, nowhere is such a man easier to find than at King Arthur's Court. Therefore do not delay; set out for Camelot immediately!"

It is easy to imagine how delighted the maiden was to hear those words.

She had her horse saddled and rode out from the courtyard like the wind. But in the first street of the town she turned back her horse, and returned secretly to the closet, to give Sir Uwaine the good news.

The Knight passed a few more days in hiding and then decided to call on the Lady of the Fountain. Again, her lovely face beneath its flood of flaming hair enchanted him and his heart rose to his throat when her greenish eyes rested upon him.

She said with some irony in her voice, "You do not seem to be at all tired after your long journey from Camelot, and not even a single grain of dust has stuck to your clothing." Then, without any further questioning, she took him by the hand, showed him round the whole castle, and finally installed him in the magnificent chamber which until quite recently had been her husband's.

Thus, Sir Uwaine gradually took the place of the Black Knight — protecting the marble fountain and winning affection in the widow's heart . . .

Exactly three years had passed since the Knight's departure from Camelot when the youthful Sir Cynon challenged his companions of the Round Table to set out in quest of Sir Uwaine, and if necessary, to avenge his death.

In full armour, Sir Kay, Sir Ban and Sir Bors, Sir Gawain, Sir Gaheris, Sir Agravain, Sir Pellinore and many others, rode forth with the pennants and shields bearing their coats-of-arms. And in command of that resplendent company was King Arthur himself, and he was more interested in Sir Uwaine's fate than anyone else.

They reached the valley with the castle of the twenty-four maidens, the one-eyed, one-legged ogre and the Fountain, by a direct path since they were led by Sir Cynon.

He was the first to pour the water from the pitcher upon the marble surrounding the Fountain and, when a horse's hooves thundered like a storm from the distance, he rode out, sword in hand, to meet the knight in black armour.

Sir Uwaine, whom none of King Arthur's Knights could recognize because of the wide shield and the helmet with the lowered visor, was much more considerate to Sir Cynon than his predecessor had been. But even so, the young Knight was soon thrown and he sustained some unpleasant bumps and bruises from his own horse.

After that, the other Knights of the Round Table also met the new Lord of the Fountain in single combat but, just like the inexperienced Sir Cynon, they also were thrown from their saddles. Before long, a remarkable number of limping Knights, as well as runaway horses, were to be seen on the plain.

In the end, it was Sir Gawain who set his spurs into the loins of his horse, Gringolet, and the Black Knight at last met his match. In the savage duel under the high fir, the double-edged swords crossed till the sparks flew from them. The turf shot out from under the horses' hooves as if fired from catapults. The other Knights, including King Arthur, watched the incredible duel with bated breath.

Then, the Black Knight knocked the sword from Sir Gawain's hand and with his own sword pressed the Knight's throat to the trunk of the fir.

And at that very moment he used his free hand to lift the visor of his helmet. It is hard to imagine the delight of the Knights of the Round Table when the invincible foe was recognized as being their erstwhile companion . . .

What remains to be added? Just that Sir Uwaine played host to the Knights of the Round Table, but refused to return to Camelot with them. It was the beauty of his wife that held him, and there were many who verified that this beauty was, indeed, not one whit inferior to that of Queen Guinevere herself!

TALE ELEVEN . . . SIR LANCELOT, SIR GARETH, AND THE RED KNIGHT . . .

How Sir Lancelot of the Lake comes to Camelot, tells of his eventful youth and becomes a Knight of the Round Table. The request of the Maid Linnet and the knighting of Beaumains. How Sir Kay the Seneschal is taught a lesson. The quest of the Red Knight and Sir Gareth's fight with him, to the death.

The adventures of Sir Gawain and Sir Uwaine were recounted at Camelot for a long, long time, and it was King Arthur who commanded that the events should be written down so as to be preserved for ever and aye.

Soon after the adventures, however, a horseman arrived at the castle, whose fame was destined to outshine the glory of Sir Gawain and all the other Knights of the Round Table. Later there would be events that were sad, very sad indeed. But everything in due time . . .

The new arrival was squarely-built and his face was manly and tanned, though he was certainly no older than Sir Gawain. Arthur, bidding him welcome, had the feeling that his face strongly reminded him of someone. So he asked, "Judging by your attire, you have come from afar. What is your name and where is your home?"

"My name is Lancelot of the Lake, Sire, but that will hardly enlighten you. You may better remember my father, King Ban of Benwick," answered the young man.

"Indeed, I remember him," exclaimed Arthur. "Thanks to your father and King Bors, we won the battle of Bedegraine Forest. Tell me how your father fares, and why I have not heard from him for such a long time."

"He is dead," replied Lancelot sadly, and as the King listened attentively, he told his story:

. . . While my father and uncle were assisting you, their enemy, King Claudas, invaded our country with a large army and laid waste to it. He even laid siege to the strong Castle Trébes, behind whose walls my mother and I were hiding.

When my father returned, he at once attacked the besiegers, but such was the strength of Claudas's men-at-arms that no sooner had he fought his way through into the castle than it was again besieged. They were out to starve us to death, and were certain to achieve this before very long.

That was why my father decided that he must get out of the castle and seek you, Sire, so that this time you might assist him in his fight.

He handed over command to his Seneschal and, under the veil of darkness, he secretly left the castle taking my mother and me with him. We got

through without problems and, when the sun rose next morning, we were resting on the shores of the lake.

111

And then it happened! My father looked back towards the castle, but what he saw instead of towers and walls was ruins and flames. Later we found out that the treacherous Seneschal had opened the gate to the enemy, who had set the castle on fire.

That horrible sight made my father lose his senses and he fell to the ground unconscious. My unhappy mother threw herself on him, but she could not restore him to life.

I sat at a distance, by the lake, and looked at the water surface. Then all of a sudden, imagine, Sire . . . the waters parted and a lovely maiden approached me. Before I knew what was happening, she had taken me by the hand and had led me down into her castle under the water.

Until quite recently she took the best care of me she could, and now she has sent me to you to become a Knight of the Round Table. She said she had once helped you, as well . . .

"She did, indeed. I am well acquainted with the Lady of the Lake," Arthur agreed. "And especially in memory of your father, it is my wish that you find Camelot a pleasant place to stay," and with these words the King hugged his new guest warmly.

All the Knights received Lancelot in their midst with good grace. He proved to be a young man who surpassed all the squires in fencing, hunting, falconry and chess. As early as Eastertide, King Arthur had decided to dub him Knight . . .

The young horseman in his glittering armour, astride his strong white horse was a fine sight. First, King Arthur girt Sir Lancelot with his sword and then, as confirmation that he was received by the brotherhood of the Round Table, he smote Sir Lancelot's bare neck with the flat of his hand. Finally a tournament was held and in this Sir Lancelot greatly distinguished himself. He struck the other Knights the greatest number of blows with both his spear and sword, he stayed longest in the saddle, and no other

113

Knight lifted the visor of his helmet later than did Sir Lancelot.

Queen Guinevere, herself, handed the victor the prize: the first of nine diamonds that King Arthur, on an expedition, had found in the coronet of an unknown dead knight. In fact the event came to be called The Diamond Tournament, and it was held annually for a period of nine years.

It was at the moment when he received the precious stone from the Queen's hands and looked into her lovely face, that Sir Lancelot vowed to himself that he would win all nine tournaments, and that he would present the diamonds to none other than Guinevere . . .

However, it was not only Lancelot who was made a Knight that year. Beaumains, who still served in the Castle kitchen, was also knighted,

and he was soon to undertake a very important quest.

Beaumains did not shirk hard work, yet even so, Sir Kay, the Seneschal, did his best to torment him. But for Sir Gawain and Sir Lancelot, he might not even have had enough to eat.

Indeed, it was Sir Lancelot who told the Seneschal, "Sir, that boy certainly is not what you take him to be. If I were you, I should take care that he doesn't seek revenge for all that rough handling."

"Do not interfere, Sir Knight, how could an ordinary scullion take his revenge on me?" laughed the Seneschal. "Perhaps with dough! But to take a real weapon in his hands, that he could never do!"

However, before long Sir Lancelot found that he had been right. One day, towards the evening, he saw Beaumains in a remote corner of the courtyard exercising with a rusty sword both thrusts and blows into a dummy figure. As the youth was going about it like a born swordsman, the Knight wasted no time in crossing arms with him, in practice.

After that Sir Lancelot coached Beaumains in secret whenever an occasion offered itself and he looked forward to the time when the overbearing Seneschal would, himself, cross arms with the youth.

Whitsuntide was drawing near and then, according to custom, knights and ladies would come to Camelot for the King to settle their quarrels or meet their various wishes, or simply to pay tribute to him.

On the very first day of the holiday, before dinner, a damsel rode into the courtyard, jumped off her horse and at once made for the banqueting hall and the Round Table. There she knelt before King Arthur and addressed him. "Your Majesty, I beseech your help for my sister, Lady Liones. The Red Knight had laid waste her lands, and now his armies are laying siege to the castle itself in revenge for her refusal to marry him. Please send one of your gallant Knights before it is too late!"

"And what is your name, noble damsel?" asked the King.

"Linnet," she answered. But before she could go on, a noise came from the Castle kitchen and, taking everyone by surprise, Beaumains took his stand before King Arthur.

"I beseech you, Sire, to hear me and to fulfil the promise you made me a year ago. Please make me a Knight and send me with the Maid Linnet to seek her sister," he asked, gasping for breath. He looked back towards the kitchen as the Seneschal appeared, shouting, "Go back, you scullion, this is not a place for you to be in!"

"Just leave him alone, dear brother, he knows why he is here," the King replied and, turning back to Beaumains he continued, "I will immediately grant both your wishes if you will tell me your real name."

"I am Gareth, Sir Gawain's youngest brother," answered the youth, at once taking a stand beside his brother for everyone to see how much alike they were.

And so King Arthur dubbed Beaumains, Sir Gareth, without heeding the Seneschal and, after dining, the newly created Knight followed the Maid Linnet out of the Castle gate.

However, it was not only the Seneschal who snubbed Beaumains, but also the high-born damsel he accompanied.

"Do not dare come close to me, Sir Scullion, I cannot bear kitchen smells!" she said angrily the moment they left the castle. "This is a true Knight the King has given me!" and with her nose turned up, she guided her horse without even looking back.

This did not worry Sir Gareth in the least; he was more concerned about leaving his lance and shield behind at Camelot and setting out into battle without them.

After a few miles a knight appeared in full armour, his spear lowered to attack. He rushed at Sir Gareth shouting, "Well, now show us what you can do, scullion! Now we shall see if the King has knighted you by rights!" By his voice it had to be the Seneschal!

Sir Gareth had hardly time to draw his sword and dip his visor, than Sir Kay charged at him furiously. Hidden behind his shield, the Seneschal hoped to unsaddle the youth with a single thrust of his long spear, but instead he himself toppled to the ground like a ripe plum.

Gareth had waited until the very last moment, when the spear had all but touched his hilt. Then he had parried the blow so violently that Sir Kay had been thrown from the saddle.

The Seneschal lay in the dust moaning, but the youth took no notice of him. He just picked up Sir Kay's shield and spear which he had come by so easily. Then, in parting, he told him, "Perhaps now you believe that the King was not mistaken, and in future you had better mind your rough manners!"

Linnet watched the whole scene, from a distance, in astonishment, but when Gareth rode up to her she sneered, "Do not think that you have won favour with me now. If God wills it, even a scullion can beat a silly knight!" Then they rode on. Linnet was in front with her nose still turned up; the Knight a good distance behind her.

When they stopped at an inn, she would not let him sit at the table with her, and it was only thanks to the innkeeper that Sir Gareth did not end up eating his meal in the straw.

The next day, however, Linnet altered her manner towards him. They were riding through a wide valley when, in the distance, they spied a lone horseman in silvery armour on a tall, white horse. Drawing nearer,

they saw that the horseman's visor was down, and he immediately challenged Sir Gareth to a duel.

It was perhaps an hour or two before the fight was over. Swords rang, shields burst, but of victory or vanquish there was none. Then the knight on the white horse lifted his visor and laughed saying, "That will do, Sir Gareth! Save your strength for the Red Knight. Though I must say that I am more than satisfied with your skill as a Knight of the Round Table."

"Oh, it is Sir Lancelot!" cried Linnet. "Is it possible that such a champion has crossed swords with a scullion?"

"No scullion," replied Sir Lancelot. "This knight is the youngest son of the King of the Orkneys and brother of Sir Gawain. It is an honour for you and your sister that he is riding to help you in your trouble. Remember that, highborn damsel!"

With those words Lancelot turned his steed. Gareth and Linnet went on their way, this time, however, side by side, with the maiden biting her lip every now and then at the thought of how she had offended the young Knight.

After riding through a fine oak forest, a strange sight met their eyes. In the wide glade in front of them stood many tents, both large and small, and in the distance rose a castle. Knights and ment-at-arms were to be seen everywhere — and, at the edge of the forest, there were forty men hanging from the oaks.

"That is the work of the Lord of the Red Plains," cried Linnet. "In such a dreadful way he has dealt with everyone willing to help my sister. I do not want you to be hanged as well, so you had better ride away from here while there is time!"

Gareth did not even listen to her. His eyes were drawn to a lone tree on which hung an ivory hunting horn, bearing a white parchment. Riding closer, he read:

BLOW THE HORN AND YOU SHALL HANG LIKE THE OTHERS

This made the youth's blood boil. To treat one's enemies like common criminals! He blew the horn so strongly and violently that the castle ramparts responded with resounding echo.

In both camp and castle, activity suddenly stopped and all eyed Sir Gareth with curiosity. Then, at one of the castle windows, a fair lady appeared and waved a white kerchief. "That is my sister, Liones," whispered Linnet.

Gareth found the Lady Liones as beautiful as the rising sun and, but for the Red Knight, he would have gazed at her in enchantment for a long time. For it was he, clad in blood-red armour on a dapple-grey horse with a scarlet caparison, who rode out to meet our hero. Sir Gareth felt like a dwarf beside him, yet he held his spear firmly. Then he rode against the Red Knight as hard as he could.

Astonished by the youth's dauntlessness, the knight laughed and in a thundering voice cried, "I see Arthur has no surplus of men-at-arms when he sends such a boy to fight me!"

Both horsemen lowered their visors and the plain echoed with the pounding of their horses' hooves. All the onlookers held their breaths. The opponents attacked furiously, crashing together with a crushing force. Both spears broke; both shields were pierced.

Then the time came for swords to be drawn, and well Gareth knew that now his life was at stake. This would be no mere entertainment as before.

The Red Knight tried to overthrow the youth as quickly as possible. His sword swished through the air like the sails of a windmill, but Gareth skilfully dodged every thrust, and few of the blows found their mark as he paid his foe back in kind.

The Red Knight realized that the fight was not going to be easy, and he fought all the more savagely. Then, he thrust his sword into Sir Gareth's shield with such force that he could not pull it out. The young Knight could have stabbed the outstretched arm but, instead, he dodged backwards, together with his shield. The Red Knight tumbled, but managed to pull Gareth down with him.

Slowly the two fighters rose from the dust; their horses had disappeared, and so there was nothing left but to continue fighting on foot. Once again the Red Knight put all his strength into every blow. Gareth jumped aside, trying to surprise his enemy, but by now they were both very tired.

There was little trace remaining of the proud shining armour. It was coated with dust and blood and naked flesh showed through in many places. The Red Knight was panting, having had to pick up his sword from the ground several times, after unsuccessful thrusts. Gareth's strength was also rapidly ebbing away; his knees sagged and he would gladly have thrown away his heavy iron plates and helmet.

Linnet stood closest to them. "Hold out, Sir Gareth, hold out!" she cried and huge tears spilled from her eyes.

Gareth heard her cry. He dropped his shield, gripped the sword with both hands and, with one last great effort, he dealt the Red Knight a tremendous blow. Then, everything dissolved before his eyes . . .

When he regained consciousness he was inside the castle. He was lying on a truly royal bed, with Linnet smiling at him on one side and her sister, the Lady Liones, on the other. They both started to tell him how, with that last blow, he had killed the Red Knight. They spoke of the great joy which had spread throughout the castle and the neighbourhood, and said that knights had been sent to take the news of the duel to King Arthur.

Sir Gareth just listened, in contentment. He did not know which of the two sisters to look at the more, since they both seemed to him equally gentle and beautiful. Nor do we know which of them he married in the end, for the ancient books are not clear about this. But all agree that he was loved by them both.

TALE TWELVE ...
THE FATE
OF MERLIN;
SIR LANCELOT
AND ELAINE ...

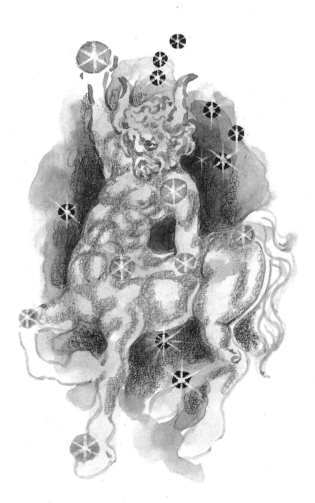

How Merlin, in his old age, falls in love with the Lady of the Lake and is imprisoned in a cave for evermore. Merlin's last prophecy. Sir Lancelot's love and torment and the Queen's jealousy. He is banished from Camelot and loses his senses. His further adventures: with Sir Bliant, with robber knights, and with a wild boar. Lancelot marries the Maid Elaine and calls himself Le Chevalier Mal Fait. Galahad is born. Sir Lancelot returns to Camelot.

When we recount the stories and adventures of the young Knights of Arthur's court, we must not forget to tell of what had befallen Merlin in his old age. The fact is, that when the gossips said that he had gone mad with love for the Lady of the Lake, they were not far from speaking the truth.

The old man had actually fallen in love with the beautiful maiden and he pursued her like a shadow wherever she went. At first the Lady of the Lake felt flattered by his courting, but after a while she began to be afraid of him. It seemed that Merlin had taken leave of his senses. He kept urging the maiden to become his wife and, when she refused, he behaved like a jealous, doting old man.

However, the Lady of the Lake was

no fool. Merlin had taught her many magic tricks and spells and now she kept wondering how to get rid of the besotted old man altogether. It was not long before a really suitable opportunity arose.

The two were riding together through the Broceliand Forest, which is thought to have been in Brittany. Reaching a glade, they saw a cave which had fallen in.

"I should like to have a look inside," said the Lady of the Lake, and Merlin replied, "Well, once would be easy, but no one could remove the caved-in rocks a second time."

Then he uttered some magic words. There was a thundering rumble and the entrance to the cave opened up.

"There is sure to be a hidden treasure inside," said the Lady of the Lake.

"I have no idea about that," answered Merlin, but the maiden insisted that he should go and find out, adding that she would then reward him with a kiss.

So, the foolish old man rushed inside. He roamed about the cave but could find no trace of any treasure. And, in the end, when he turned back there was a thunderous rumble, the rocks came rolling down and the cave fell in again!

This was the work of the Lady of the Lake; in vain Merlin begged her to let him out. All he met with was mockery, "Didn't you say yourself that no one could open the cave a second time? So why did you go inside, you foolish old man?" With those words the Lady of the Lake leapt on her horse and dashed out of the forest.

As for Merlin, he thundered at the top of his voice until, at last, he realized it was all in vain and he was fated to stay in the cave for ever . . .

Indeed, at Camelot, it did appear that the earth had swallowed up the old counsellor, even though the Court did not know his fate.

The twelve candles on the grave of King Lot burned with just a small flickering flame, and so Arthur ordered a search to be made for Merlin.

The Knights of the Round Table rode out and it was Sir Gawain who happened to find himself in Broceliand. He was in no hurry, and gave Gringolet an entirely free rein so that his steed sought his own way through the deep forest. Just as it began to grow dark, Gawain rode into the glade where the cave had fallen in. For some strange reason, the spot held a peculiar attraction for him; even Gringolet pricked his ears and would not budge from there.

"Is there anybody here?" shouted the Knight as loud as he could.

And then a familiar voice came from the depths of the cave, "Here I am, but no one can help me any more . . . give my message to the King!"

Sir Gawain recognized Merlin's voice and shouted to ask him what had happened. The old man told him the

whole story, truthfully, and then gave his prophecy:

... The stars show that a misfortune will befall Camelot. A hatred will occur among the Knights of the Round Table, and only the Holy Grail will be able to free them from those sufferings. But for how long I do not know ...

Then Merlin fell silent. Even though Sir Gawain strongly urged him to explain his mysterious prophecy, the old man did not utter another word.

When Sir Gawain returned to Camelot and told the story of Merlin's fate and his peculiar prophecy, the King frowned deeply, and many a Knight began to wonder what the future had in store for him.

But, as time passed, the whole incident became forgotten. The Knights rode out on distant war expeditions and experienced glorious adventures as before.

Sir Lancelot was the only man who could not forget Merlin's last words. He was hiding from all the others what he was unable to disclose to anyone, and that was his burning passion for Queen Guinevere.

From the moment when he had first seen the Queen and she had given him her first smile, that feeling had burnt more and more ardently in his heart. Then, one day when they were alone together in the flower garden, Sir Lancelot openly revealed his love for Guinevere.

The Queen was not surprised, for she herself had cherished the Knight in her thoughts for a long time. And,

123

on that evening, the two kissed for the first time and vowed to remain faithful to each other till death.

However, what had, to begin with, filled them both with happiness, was to become a source of great torment to Lancelot. He still could not confide in anybody and his greatest worry was that he was betraying the King. Arthur esteemed him beyond all the other Knights of the Round Table and, to show his favour, had the Castle of the Joyous Gard built, which he bestowed upon Sir Lancelot as a gift.

Lancelot took Merlin's last prophecy, as announced by Sir Gawain, to refer to himself and he avoided Camelot, preferring to make long journeys, looking for fights and dangers. In spite of this, his love for, and memories of, Guinevere pursued him everywhere. Again and again he had to return, just to see her lovely face and to hear her voice — if only for a brief time.

And so, while rumours spread that Lancelot was the bravest and best fighter in the world who avoided no encounter and always came out triumphant, there was nothing but sadness in the Knight's heart because of his secret love for the Queen.

One day, whilst he was staying at Camelot, Elaine, the beautiful daughter of King Pelles of Carbonek, paid a visit to the Castle. She pretended to have stopped there by chance during her journey to London but, in fact, the visit was well planned.

Not quite a week before, as the maiden had celebrated her sixteenth birthday, her father had let her into the following secret. "At your birth, dear Elaine," he had said, "the weird sisters prophesied that you will give birth to a son who will gain the most precious thing in the world — the Holy Grail. The best knight of Britain will be his father."

"And why are you telling me this now?" asked Elaine wonderingly.

"It is time you got to know your bridegroom," answered King Pelles. "Certainly Sir Lancelot is the finest knight of them all and, if you are lucky, you will find him now at the Royal Castle of Camelot." He continued, "There is one piece of advice you should not forget — be sure not to tell anybody the reason for your visit. There are many who would try to upset everything."

Elaine remembered her father's advice and no one had an inkling of why she had come to Camelot. Since she was as fair and fresh as the rising sun, all the Knights paid court to her; even old Sir Ector gave her a smile whenever his eyes rested on her.

Only Sir Lancelot ignored her, even though she tried to gain his interest. But the Queen soon became aware of Elaine's intent and, instead of the kindness she had first shown, she became full of jealousy and hatred.

Elaine bore Lancelot's lack of interest with great pain. The attraction she

had felt for the Knight was growing from day to day until, very soon, she fell hopelessly in love with him. And it was then that she confided in her young chambermaid, Brisen, asking her advice.

Brisen was very fond of her mistress and, wishing to help her, she quickly devised a plan. She would arrange a meeting between Elaine and Sir Lancelot in some remote corner of the royal garden where they could talk undisturbed.

But all had been disclosed to the Queen and hardly had the Knight greeted the blushing Elaine than Guinevere appeared, fuming with anger. "So much for those vows of yours to keep faith with me!" she ranted and raved at Lancelot. "Is this how you keep your word as a Knight? Get out of my sight! Go, and never show your face at Camelot again!"

Sir Lancelot turned deathly pale, gasped several times without uttering a sound and then, as if bereft of his senses, turned and ran out of the garden, out of the castle — until the forests on the horizon swallowed him up.

Guinevere paid no heed to this, but screamed again, this time at the Maid Elaine, "And you get out of my sight, too!"

"I shall be glad to, but there is something I must say before I go," said the maiden looking Guinevere straight in the face. "But for you, Lancelot might have fallen in love with me. And when you have the best king in the world for your husband, why do you still demand the love of another?" Saying this Elaine left the garden. The Queen remained where she was; she let her head drop into her hands and she started to weep.

Guinevere wept and wept and was not to be comforted. Only in the evening did her tears dry. At once she started wondering how to put right all the harm she had done by her jealousy, and what to do to make Sir Lancelot return. After much thought, she chose three trusty Knights and sent them to search for him . . . . .

And what was happening to Sir Lancelot in the meantime?

When he fled from Camelot to the forest, he behaved as if he really had lost his reason. He made his way through the thickets until a torn shirt was all that was left of his clothing. Then, on he went through the forest, and away from the Castle, not knowing where he was going. Perhaps for a whole month, even a year, he rambled on, living on roots and berries. His face became overgrown with a stubble of a beard, and the rags of his shirt hardly covered his emaciated body.

Then, one day, he came to a glade where there stood a coloured silk tent. A white shield and two swords hung on a branch beside it. When Lancelot saw this, he rushed forward with a great cry and snatched one of the

swords, smiting and stabbing at the shield until chips and splinters flew in all directions.

Some moments later the hangings of the tent were drawn apart and a stalwart knight in armour appeared, accompanied by a dwarf. "Why are you trying to destroy my shield?" he yelled angrily at the man wearing nothing but a shirt.

Sir Lancelot turned round. "Do not come near me!" he answered menacingly, and struck the shield such a blow that he cut it in two.

The knight became extremely angry. "Now come and attack me!" he cried, drawing his sword.

At first Lancelot seemed not to have heard him. But, when the knight drew closer, he seized the sword with both

was echoing with Lancelot's heavy snoring.

"Whatever has happened to me?" said the knight sitting up and fingering the sizable bump on his head, "I feel as if a rock has crashed down on me!"

"The madman in shirt-sleeves did it, my lord," the dwarf reminded Sir Bliant, "and then he fled to your tent and fell asleep. Can't you hear him snoring?"

For a while Sir Bliant listened to the sounds issuing from the tent, and then he decided, "Now I can repay him for the blow. I shall go and kill him; I shall show him no mercy."

"I would not do that, my lord.

hands and used it like a bludgeon to strike a savage blow to the knight's helmet.

The crazed Lancelot's sword broke into pieces and the attacked knight fell down into the grass, unconscious. Then, to the amazement of the watching dwarf, Sir Lancelot entered the tent, lay down on a pile of furs, and at once fell asleep.

Before the dwarf had managed to bring the knight, Sir Bliant (for such was his name) back to life, the glade

128

Although he seems to be a madman, his face seems familiar to me," said the dwarf.

Sir Bliant realized that his servant was speaking wisely, so he entered the tent quietly so as not to wake the sleeper. The moment he saw him at close quarters he recognized him. Indeed, this was Sir Lancelot, who had recently triumphed in the jousting at the Castle of Lonazep!

So the knight tiptoed out and, together with the dwarf, made a horse litter. On it they placed the sleeping Lancelot, and conveyed him to Sir Bliant's castle.

Here Lancelot lived for more than a year, but he did not recover his senses, nor did he speak a word to anyone. Although he was fed and clothed as befits a high-born guest, his hands and feet were bound with strong chains so he could harm no one in an attack of madness.

One day Lancelot, still in his chains, was looking out of a castle window when out of the nearby forest ran Sir Bliant. He had lost his horse and was being pursued and attacked by two robber knights on horseback.

Using all his strength, Lancelot tore off his chains and rushed from the castle. Before the robbers had time to recover from their surprise, Lancelot threw one of them from his horse and flung him to the ground so ferociously that the soul left the robber's body. The other did not wait for his turn. He

spurred his horse and ran for his life. So, Lancelot saved his host from certain death.

From that day Sir Bliant held Sir Lancelot in high esteem and, although the guest remained disturbed in his mind, he was allowed to move about quite freely.

Not long after, Lancelot set out for a walk in the forest, but before long he

130

got lost and could not find his way back to the castle. Instead he came to a small hermitage and what should he see but an old hermit defending himself with a long stick against the attack of a huge wild boar!

Without hesitating, Sir Lancelot gripped his sword and felled the beast with a blow to its head. But when he approached the animal, thinking it dead, the boar buried its tusks, which were sharp as knives, in his thigh. Overcoming his pain, Sir Lancelot dealt yet another blow with his sword, and this time killed the boar.

For days, Lancelot lay in the hermitage and the holy man treated him with herb applications. The wounds

131

healed quickly, but Lancelot lost strength since the hermit's fare was simple and not sufficiently nourishing for him. But at least he partly retained his senses and one day, when the hermit was away, Lancelot escaped.

Again, he could not find the way to the castle of the good Sir Bliant. However, he did emerge from the forest after several days, and soon saw a town and a mighty castle. This was the town of Carbonek, where King Pelles ruled and where he lived with the fair Maid Elaine. But Lancelot had forgotten everything and everybody, even Elaine and Queen Guinevere. In fact, the only people he remembered were Sir Bliant and the old hermit.

As he walked through the streets of Carbonek barefoot and in rags, boys jumped about him, shouting, "A fool! A fool! Look at the fool!"

But Sir Lancelot walked on as if he had not heard them. Only when the street urchins began to throw stones at him from all sides, did he take to his heels in confusion.

He might have been killed but for two young squires who took up the blood-stained Knight and led him to the castle. There they treated his wounds and washed him, dressing him in clean clothing. And Lancelot, having eaten his fill, fell into a sound sleep on the straw where the servants slept at night.

The squires decided that Lancelot might be of noble birth, and so they ran to tell King Pelles what had happened. But they first met his daughter, Elaine, and took her along to see their unknown fool.

So it happened that the maiden found her Knight again, after a long separation. Though he never recognized her, he soon fell in love with her and made her his wife. King Pelles had a small castle built for them on an island in the river and since Lancelot had even forgotten his own name, he called himself Le Chevalier Mal Fait, meaning The Knight who has Trespassed. Then, before a year had passed, Elaine gave birth to a son, as the weird sisters had foretold, and she named him Galahad . . .

Though Lancelot did not regain his memory, he soon regained his knightly skills. He won easy victories at tournaments and, after a time, he proclaimed a contest on his own island.

Knights from far and near came riding there, many having come from faraway countries. And then, the three trusty knights sent by Queen Guinevere to search for Lancelot and bring him back to Camelot, appeared on the island. At once they went to pay tribute to the Chevalier Mal Fait, and how amazed they were to see before them the man for whom they had been searching!

Even Lancelot himself was dumbfounded at the sight of those familiar faces and, at that very moment, he suddenly recalled King Arthur's Court and the way the Queen had driven him out. An immense desire for her flooded his heart.

The visitors, as though suspecting what was in Sir Lancelot's mind, told him that Guinevere was sorry for what she had done, and that everyone wanted him to return.

However, Sir Lancelot had doubts. It was not his fault that he had lost his memory, but he could not just abandon Elaine because he was more attracted by the prospect of returning to Camelot.

At that moment Elaine came into the hall, and she knew at once what had happened. And, though sorrow drove tears into her eyes, she bade Lancelot go!

So, having bidden farewell to the sad Elaine and to his little son Galahad, the celebrated Sir Lancelot of the Lake was, after three years, on his way back to the Round Table.

TALE THIRTEEN... TRISTRAM AND ISOLDE

Wholly devoted to Sir Tristram, starting with his birth, the poisoned cup, his first combat with Sir Marhaus and how both suffer heavy wounds. Tristram goes to Ireland and meets Isolde. About King Mark's wooing and Tristram's fight on behalf of the King of Ireland. Who drinks the love potion and why Tristram becomes a knight-errant. He goes to Brittany to try to forget his love for Queen Isolde. Tristram's sickness and the sad end of the two lovers.

As already told, it was after three long years that Sir Lancelot returned to Camelot. All the Knights of the Round Table rejoiced greatly and Queen Guinevere was delighted. Once again the Castle was full of good cheer and merry-making, and time passed quickly. However, let us now leave Camelot, for this eventful and very sad story...

There were two kings in the far south-west of Britain. They lived in peace and good neighbourliness and acknowledged Arthur as the supreme ruler. King Meliodas reigned in the country of Lyonesse, which, today, is covered by the seas, and King Mark had Cornwall under his sceptre.

Meliodas had married King Mark's

sister, and after several years of marriage she gave birth to a son. He was a handsome little boy, but his mother had suffered so much pain in her pregnancy and shed so many tears that she died not long afterwards. However, before she died she gave him the name of Tristram, which means 'of sorrowful birth'.

Several years passed and Meliodas married again. At first the new Queen was quite fond of Tristram, but when her own sons were born, she began to wonder how to get rid of him so that he, being the first-born, should not become King after Meliodas's death.

In the end, she decided to poison Tristram. In secret she dripped poison into his cup of wine. But the plan went badly wrong! It was the Queen's own son who drank the wine down to the dregs and, after suffering terrible pains, he died.

Tristram's stepmother was not discouraged by the disaster. She wanted Tristram's death even more, and once again she prepared a poisoned potion.

This time she kept her eyes on it constantly but, instead of Tristram, it was the King who took the cup. As he was on the point of drinking, the Queen jumped to his side, tore the cup out of his hand, and emptied out the wine. "Do not drink it, for God's sake! Do not drink it!" she cried.

At first Meliodas looked at her in complete astonishment, but then it dawned on him what had happened.

"You were trying to poison Tristram, you wretch!" he said in horror.

At first, the Queen denied it, but eventually, with tears in her eyes, she confessed her crime.

Meliodas didn't think twice; the Queen must be burnt at the stake! The fire was already burning when Tristram fell on his knees before his father and said, "Father, there is just one request I want you to grant me. . ."

"Do not be timid," the King cut him short. "You know full well that I shall be glad to grant you any request."

"So spare the Queen's life! Please!" begged Tristram.

Meliodas was furious, but he was unable to refuse his son. "You are a fool," he said. "Don't you realize that she wanted to kill you just to help her own sons?"

"I know that, but I have forgiven her, and my wish is that you also will bear her no ill will," answered Tristram, very seriously.

The King agreed to grant his plea and, from then on, they all dwelt in happiness and contentment, for the Queen bestowed her favour upon her stepson beyond others and did everything to please and protect him.

When Tristram was getting on for nineteen, Anguish, King of Ireland, took it into his head that he must receive a tribute in gold from Tristram's uncle, King Mark of Cornwall, or he would send an army into the country.

The ruler of Cornwall was not frightened. He answered Anguish immediately and challenged him to send

his bravest knight to triumph in a duel. Only then would he get the demanded tribute.

Anguish did not delay. He sent Sir Marhaus, by ship, to the shores of Cornwall. Sir Marhaus was indeed a good warrior and one of the Knights of the Round Table. In addition, he had recently become brother-in-law to King Anguish.

Though right was on his side, King Mark did not find anyone willing to champion his cause. Indeed, when the tidings of Sir Marhaus spread through Cornwall, no man was found there bold enough to cross arms with him.

Young Tristram heard the news too, and though not yet a knight, he and his squire, Gouvernail, set out immediately to help his uncle.

King Mark was more than pleased with his nephew's bravery, since he had begun to fear that he would have to fight Sir Marhaus himself; a prospect he did not savour in the least. He, therefore, made haste to knight Tristram and, according to custom, presented him with armour, weapons and a horse. Then, that very day, he sent him, with Gouvernail, to the shore.

The two arrived just in time. The ship had landed, and Sir Marhaus was already astride his stocky dapple-grey horse. Seeing Tristram, he asked, "Do not tell me that King Mark has sent you to fight the duel? Be advised and ride home, for I do not feel like killing

such an inexperienced young knight!"

"I am not afraid of you, and at least I shall have a chance to gain that experience you speak about!" said Tristram, lowering his visor.

So Sir Marhaus, too, lowered his

visor and the adversaries drew their swords and charged. At the very first blow they were both thrown, and Sir Marhaus had wounded Tristram in the side.

The young knight did not notice the wound at first. He rose nimbly and once again engaged in the fight. Sir Marhaus realized that his opponent was far from being as defenceless as he had thought. What Tristram lacked in experience and strength he made up for in dexterity and speed. One moment he was here, the next he was there, and so his opponent's random blows mostly just cut the air.

Then, when they had fought for more than two hours, Tristram dealt Marhaus a blow to the helmet with his sword. The blade penetrated the plate and Sir Marhaus fell, unconscious. The duel was over. The Irishmen carried their knight back to the ship and set out for home under full sail.

138

Only then did Tristram become aware that blood was oozing from his side and that he was feeling very weak. But, with Gouvernail's help, he got into the saddle again and rode to King Mark's Castle to tell him of the victory.

The King was overjoyed, especially since, now, he did not have to pay the Irish King the tribute he had demanded. He bestowed all possible care on Tristram so that his wound would heal as quickly as possible. Tristram lay in bed and whiled away the time with music, playing the harp, although his wound still gave him pain . . .

But what had happened to Sir Marhaus in the meantime? He had managed to get back to his native Ireland and to the castle of King Anguish, but he died from his terrible injury a few days later.

Sir Marhaus's sister—the Queen of Ireland—swore to avenge his death. In her brother's head had been found a piece of Tristram's sword, and this the Queen kept . . .

Tristram was doing little better. At King Mark's Castle, the physicians and herbalists attended him constantly but the young knight grew worse and worse, week after week.

Then, an ancient herbalist told him, "There is poison, deep in your wound, because Sir Marhaus's sword was envenomed. But it is not within my power to get rid of it. Only in Ireland do they know the cure, and only there can you find help."

Tristram accepted the advice and asked King Mark to send him by sailing ship to Ireland.

Landed in that country, the young man took lodgings not far from King Anguish's Castle and, from the first day, played such enchanting and moving tunes on his harp that both simple folk and noblemen from the whole neighbourhood gathered under his window to listen.

Before long the melodies enticed Isolde, King Anguish's daughter, who was said to be the fairest maid in the whole of Ireland. Moreover, Isolde surpassed all in her knowledge of how to treat wounds and diseases.

The magic music gave her no rest. She tried to find out from where the unknown knight came, but all she could learn was that he was tormented by an incurable wound in his side. She decided that Tristram should be brought to the Royal Castle, where she could take care of him herself. There, she tended him, day and night, until he recovered.

Meanwhile, everybody in the Castle had come to like Tristram. Only the Queen did not trust him, and one day she secretly stole into his chamber. At once she found that her feelings were justified: the edge of the young man's sword lacked exactly that piece that she had found in her dying brother's head. She rushed to King Anguish and demanded that he would have Tristram put to the sword.

Anguish agreed, to calm her, but he was not seeking revenge, for he knew that Tristram had overcome the Queen's brother in an equal and honourable fight. In the end, he sent Isolde to warn the youth that he would lose his life unless he left Ireland quickly.

Tristram did not delay. At the break of dawn his ship left Ireland. He had saved his life and yet he was sad to be going, because while dwelling at King Anguish's Castle, he had fallen in love with the fair Isolde and could not forget her. And although he was quite unaware of it, Isolde has also fallen for him and ardently wished to meet him again.

King Mark had long become reconciled to the death of his nephew, so he was much astonished to see Tristram return fit and well. Without waiting to be asked, Tristram recounted what he had experienced in Ireland and he was, of course, most enthusiastic about the fair and wise Isolde.

His uncle listened to him with envy and, before many weeks had passed, an unexpected idea came into his mind.

"It is high time that I, too, got married," he said to Tristram one day. "I know of no suitable bride myself, but you have praised Isolde so much that she is sure to prove the perfect bride for me. And, as for you, it will be child's play for you to bring her quickly to Cornwall."

Tristram was flabbergasted but,

having always been obedient to his uncle, he promised to do what he asked. What King Mark most desired was that Tristram should never return to his Castle, but the youth did not suspect this.

Tristram was fully aware of the danger that threatened him in Ireland but, even so, he was eager to set out as soon as possible. He had the wedding gifts from King Mark loaded on to the vessel, and his only companion was to be his faithful squire, Gouvernail.

They set sail early in the morning with the sun shining and a favourable wind blowing, but no sooner had the shore vanished from their sight, than an icy north wind arose. In a moment, the sky was covered with pitch-black clouds and the thunder rolled. Giant waves tossed the sailing ship at their will, the gale tore off the sails, and a zigzag of lightning split the mast in two.

All that night, and then for the next twenty days and nights, the seas raged. It was a miracle that no one was drowned.

Dawn of the twenty-first day of the voyage arrived. The ship had stopped rolling and was heading for a nearby coast which was emerging from the morning mist.

"Southampton! We are in England!" shouted the sailors, having recognized the familiar harbour.

Having landed, Tristram followed his squire's advice and set out for near-

fight a duel with Sir Blamor. He does not seem to be too keen to engage in the battle, for Sir Blamor is a cousin of Sir Lancelot and so is a good swordsman!"

"I might help King Anguish by fighting instead of him," suggested Tristram.

Arthur shrugged his shoulders and said, "But Sir Blamor is a more formidable opponent than Sir Marhaus. You should not forget that."

The next day King Anguish was surprised to see Tristram, but when the youth suggested he would take his place in the duel, he gratefully accepted the offer.

And so in the presence of King Arthur and the other Knights of the Round Table, the opponents mounted their steeds, set their spears, and charged against each other. The thrust was heavy but while Tristram did not budge in his saddle, Sir Blamor tumbled to the ground. His lance had broken, his horse had fled, and he was entirely at his opponent's mercy.

"Will you yield?" asked Tristram, aiming his spear at the prostrate knight.

"I will not beg you to spare my life," answered Sir Blamor, gritting his teeth and awaiting his end.

However, instead of striking, Tristram helped the vanquished knight to his feet, and from that moment he won not only his favour but Sir Lancelot's as well.

by Camelot. In the meantime the ship was to be repaired in the port.

King Arthur gave the knight a kind welcome. All night he listened to his adventures as well as an account of the mission with which he had been entrusted by his uncle.

When Tristram had finished, Arthur said with an amused smile, "You are afraid of King Anguish, and he in turn is afraid of me. He is staying at Camelot with his Queen and with Princess Isolde, and tomorrow he is expected to

No less gratified was King Anguish himself. He never referred to the duel with Sir Marhaus but promised to grant any wish that Tristram might express.

What other could the young knight wish but the hand of Isolde for his uncle, though his heart bled when he said so. Everybody was surprised to hear such a request and most surprised of all was Isolde. Indeed, she had always hoped that Tristram would come back to claim her for himself, and now she was to become the wife of an old man she had never even seen!

Nevertheless, King Anguish was a man of his word. So Tristram had the wedding gifts brought over from Southampton, and ordered the ship to be got ready for the return voyage to Cornwall.

On that voyage Isolde was to be accompanied only by her nurse Bragwain who had tended the maiden since her childhood and had grown extremely fond of her. And it was Bragwain whom the Queen came to see shortly before departure. She carried a small

wickered flask and said, "I know Isolde does not want to marry the man chosen for her. Therefore, I have brought this love potion. When you pour it into King Mark's and my daughter's cups during the wedding, they will fall in love for ever, and it will be a happy marriage. But I must warn you, do not let anyone else touch the potion!"

Bragwain assured the Queen that she would act according to her wishes,

and not long afterwards Tristram's ship sailed from Southampton.

There was a strong gale blowing, so they sailed close in to the coast. Isolde stayed with Bragwain in her cabin, and Tristram did not appear, though he longed to see the damsel he loved.

Towards the evening the gale died down. The ship was silently sailing towards the setting sun, and it was then that the young couple met after all. Isolde was standing at the gunwale

144

sadly contemplating the passing waters and quietly shedding not a few tears, when Tristram suddenly appeared, and said, "Look at the havoc the gale has wrought!" And indeed, there was much still lying about the deck which had come loose through the perpetual swaying or had fallen from boxes. "There is even some good wine lying here," said Isolde, pointing at the wickered flask.

Tristram wondered how the flask had got there and what it contained. So he picked it up, uncorked it and took a draught. Indeed, it did contain wine, but it was so unusual and delicious that he said to Isolde, "Come and taste it! I'm sure you've never tasted such good wine before."

An hour later Bragwain too came out on deck to find her ward, and immediately she saw what had happened. The flask was lying empty and, under the mast, Tristram and Isolde were in each other's arms.

"They have drunk the magic potion," whispered Bragwain and crossed herself in terror. Then she hurried to tell Gouvernail what happened.

As for Tristram and Isolde, the potion enchanted them to the end of their days. A deep love for each other sprang up and there was no power that could set them free of it.

Even so, Bragwain and Gouvernail contrived to arrange things so that King Mark did not notice anything amiss. He married Isolde, and even wanted his nephew to remain in Cornwall. However, the clever Gouvernail managed to persuade Tristram to reject the invitation. "It will be better for you, sir, if we leave here and you do not see Isolde," he said. "Believe me, you will find it easier to forget her and, who knows, you may find a damsel whom you will take to your heart even more."

Thus it happened that Tristram became a knight-errant, a knight who wandered in search of adventure. He would often stay at Camelot, where he made friends with Sir Lancelot, won many tournaments and even overthrew Sir Palomides, the celebrated Saracen knight. But he became perhaps even more renowned for his harp playing and his sad songs, for in these alone was he able to express his infinite longing for his beloved Isolde.

For months, even years, Tristram travelled with Gouvernail from place to place. Then, one day, his squire spoke to him. "I know well what has been vexing you, my lord and, believe me, my heart goes out to you. Wherever you go you think of Isolde because Cornwall is near," he said. "Let us, instead, go overseas. I have some good friends in Brittany and a different country with different people may rid you of your great torment."

The knight listened to Gouvernail, nodded sadly and then begged him, "I know you are right and I will follow your advice. But I must see Isolde once again before we sail. It may be for the last time."

As ever, the squire was ready to help Tristram. They rode to Cornwall and, once there, Gouvernail learnt from Bragwain where Queen Isolde was wont to walk, so that Tristram might wait for her there. Bragwain warned against such a meeting, saying that King Mark was suspicious, but Gouvernail kept this to himself.

Brief are the moments of bliss and of sunshine, long is the night and despair in a man's life. Like a fleeting dream, the moment passed when Tristram held Isolde in his arms and heard from her lips that she still loved him. Then, he boarded ship for the sailing to Brittany.

Sir Ganhardin with whom they stayed, in Brittany, was a cheerful and hearty fellow. He provided much entertainment for his guests. There were frequent hunts as well as fishing, and merchants and jugglers would visit from all over the world.

Tristram was esteemed by one and all, particularly by Sir Ganhardin's sister who had eyes only for the young knight. She was a happy, black-haired maiden and, strange to tell, her name also was Isolde, but because of her beautiful slim hands and snow-white complexion, she was generally called Isolde of the White Hands.

Though Tristram was friendly to everyone, the black-haired maiden soon realized how sad he was. Often,

in secret, she had listened to him singing and playing the harp. Although she did not understand the words, she believed he was singing about her — having heard her name mentioned several times in the songs.

However, before her mistake could be discovered, something dreadful happened. Brittany was struck by an unknown sickness and no one knew the cure. Three days after falling ill, people died — in their hundreds. Sir Ganhardin took every care to prevent the disease from spreading to his estates but, even so, Tristram was the first to fall sick from it.

He knew only too well that there was no cure for the disease, so he called Gouvernail to his bedside and told him, "In three days I am fated to die, and the only person who can cure me is Queen Isolde. She has already cured me once before. Will you go and fetch her, Gouvernail?"

"Of course, my lord, but the journey is long and King Mark will hardly allow Queen Isolde to visit you. You see, he has heard about your love for each other!" answered the squire.

Tristram thought for a while and then, propping himself up on his elbows, he whispered through feverish lips, "I shall be waiting at the port to see whether Isolde is coming. But make sure that your ship has white sails if she is on board. If they are black, I shall know she is not with you." Having said this, he dropped down on the pillow exhausted, and closed his eyes.

Gouvernail left the chamber on tip-toes. He asked the black-haired Isolde to convey Tristram to the port and to look out for a ship with white sails, which would arrive in three days' time. Then he set sail for Cornwall himself.

That very afternoon the ailing knight was carried over into a fisher-man's cottage which had a fine view across the sea. Isolde of the White Hands took the best care of him that she could, but Tristram was more and more plagued by the fever.

He became delirious, and from his rambling words the maiden learnt the whole story of Tristram's love for the golden-haired Queen Isolde and why they were waiting for a ship with white sails. She was bitterly disappointed that Tristram's love was not for her but, nevertheless, she did not leave his bedside.

The third day arrived. The fever had left him, but the knight was so weak that he could not even speak. Only with considerable effort could he turn his eyes towards the window, silently asking if Gouvernail's ship was yet in sight.

When the bells in the village began to strike noon, the maiden espied a mast on the horizon. "A ship is coming," she said hollowly, feeling the tears in her eyes. Then, through the veil of these tears, she saw the snow-white rigging.

Tristram asked weakly, but with hope, "And what colour are the sails?"

"Black," lied Isolde of the White Hands, without knowing why she did so.

Tristram was silent, and when she moved to his bedside she saw that he had died. In despair she cried out aloud and did not even notice that the door had flown open with a clang.

There, on the threshold, stood Queen Isolde and Gouvernail. The maiden glanced up and sobbed, "You are late, too late. . ."

The golden-haired Queen slowly approached the bed to give her beloved Tristram one last kiss. However, the moment she touched his cold lips, her heart broke in sorrow, and she fell, dead, beside him. . .

Such, then is the end of the story of the great love between the fairest princess of Ireland, Isolde, and the knight, Sir Tristram, born in sorrow and pain.

TALE FOURTEEN . . .
PERCIVAL AND
THE BLACK KNIGHT;
SIR GERAINT
AND ENID . . .

The hunt for the White Stag and how the Queen oversleeps and suffers double insults. The arrival of Percival, and his victory over the Black Knight. How Sir Geraint pursues the Falcon Knight, encounters the Knight's uncle and cousin Enid, and avenges the Queen. Sir Geraint decides to make Enid his bride. Arthur meets Sir Geraint and Percival in the forest and Sir Kay is taught another lesson.

The news of the tragic fate of Tristram and Isolde soon spread to all the towns and castles, carried by wandering minstrels. Later the story came to be recorded in many books.

But let us return to Camelot, where preparations for a great hunt were under way. Indeed, a White Stag had been sighted in the woods around the Castle, and the King resolved to hold a chase for it. Both Arthur and his Knights yearned for the rare trophy, and the Queen said, on the eve of the hunt, "I should also like to join in the spectacle this time. Are you going to take me with you?"

"Why, of course," said Arthur with a smile. "But we shall have to set out early in the morning and we won't wait for anybody."

she had her white horse saddled and, taking with her a young chambermaid, she rode out from the gate.

It was a sunny day; the horses were trotting side by side, and the air was sweet with fragrance. The trail left by the huntsmen was not difficult to follow and, in a clearing, the Queen soon saw a familiar fair-haired horseman. "Oh, there is Sir Geraint," she said to her companion. "Do call to him!"

Sir Geraint had recently come to Camelot, from Devon, and he was a great favourite with the Queen's maids and ladies-in-waiting. He joined Guinevere, and the three of them rode on.

Hardly had they spoken, when they came across a tall knight and a damsel crossing their path in the forest. Following the couple was a bearded dwarf, running for all he was worth.

"Who are they? I have never seen the knight or the damsel before now," said Guinevere wonderingly.

"I do not know." Sir Geraint shrugged his shoulders.

The Queen dismounted and, coming up to the dwarf, asked, "Tell me the name of your lord."

"That's none of your business," snapped the bearded dwarf, ungraciously.

Guinevere, as if not noticing his rudeness, said, "Well, I shall have to ask him myself, since I shall learn nothing from you."

The dwarf turned red with rage and

In spite of his warning, Guinevere, as usual, did not rise till late in the morning. The huntsmen had long since gone, and there was no one left in the Castle but the servants and Sir Kay the Seneschal.

Guinevere was furious and decided to ride into the forest on her own. So then slapped the Queen's face so violently that she staggered. He mumbled something under his breath and, without hurrying, set off to join his master.

The poor Queen returned to the others, in tears. "I will get even with that ill-mannered dwarf, and with the knight!" cried Sir Geraint, who had watched the whole scene. And he ran in pursuit of the dwarf.

Guinevere had, by now, lost all inclination to find the hunters and so turned back for Camelot.

At home another unpleasant surprise awaited her so, instead of following Geraint, we shall stay with the Queen for the moment.

Guinevere found it hard to recover from the dwarf's insulting behaviour. No sooner had her maids helped her to undress than she ordered a cup of wine to be brought, to give her at least some good cheer. She was on the point of taking the cup when, suddenly, a wild-looking knight in black armour appeared in the hall. He seized the cup and dashed the wine into the Queen's face. "I shall wait in the meadow below the Castle till some of the exceedingly brave Knights of the

and wiped her cheeks with her hands. Only when the maids rushed to her aid did she burst out crying.

Before long, having heard the Queen's lamentations, Sir Kay appeared in the hall. He listened to Guinevere's complaints and rushed down to the courtyard hoping to find the intruder still there. But there was no trace of him anywhere.

However, an extraordinary sight met the Seneschal's eyes. In the middle of the courtyard stood a dapple-grey horse. Actually, it looked more like the skeleton of a horse covered with a dapple-grey hide. The animal had no saddle or harness. Its young rider held himself proudly and erect, though his clothes were poor and patched and a piece of string served him as a belt.

"Who are you and what do you want here?" Sir Kay addressed him sternly.

The unknown horseman looked at him and said, "My name is Percival. My mother has sent me to seek King Arthur."

"What important message are you bringing to the King?" asked the Seneschal.

"I want him to make me a knight . . ." Percival had not even finished speaking before Sir Kay broke into a loud laughter.

"You? Such a ragamuffin? Indeed, I could never have imagined anyone so arrogant!"

Sir Kay might have thundered on

Round Table come to challenge me to a duel. He who overthrows me will get the cup back!" he laughed. And in a moment he was gone.

Guinevere gasped for breath, unable to utter a sound. She stood looking unbelievingly at her stained garments had it not been for the King's two jesters who appeared in the courtyard at that moment. They started chanting with one accord, "Long live Sir Percival, the best knight in the world! Long may he live!"

"Shut up!" the Seneschal snapped at them, and gave them each a box on the ears. So heavy were the blows that the two jesters began crying loudly and then started turning somersaults in the courtyard.

"I have never met such a rude man," commented Percival. "When I become a knight, I shall punish you on behalf of those poor wretches."

Sir Kay only laughed. "And how do you expect to become a knight? You have no sword, no spear, no armour . . ." he started to say.

"What are they?" inquired the youth, in such a simple-minded way that the Seneschal could not help laughing heartily.

"You are even ignorant of that? Well, in the meadow under the castle, a knight in black armour is waiting with a well-pointed sword and a sharp

spear. If you overthrow him, you may take them all and his horse with a good saddle, as well."

"Sound advice at last," answered Percival, and, turning round his poor horse, he rode towards the gate and then made for the meadow.

The knight in the black armour could not believe his eyes when he saw young Percival. "Do not tell me they have sent you down from the Castle?" he asked.

Percival nodded and said, "I am supposed to fight you to win your armour. Otherwise they say I cannot become a knight. So, get ready!" And the youth spurred his horse and urged it into a trot against his opponent.

When the Black Knight saw the motley pile of rags and bones approaching him and the horseman waving his arms threateningly, he drew his sword and waited.

Then, the dapple-grey horse ambled up to him, and suddenly reared up on its hind legs. Before the knight could raise his shield to defend himself, he received such a blow from the horse's hooves that he tumbled to the ground, unconscious.

By that time, Sir Kay had become curious about what was happening to that silly youth. So he had himself dressed in armour and, mounting his horse, gingerly rode towards the meadow.

But what he saw in the distance was so incredible that, in his confusion, he

turned his steed back to the Castle gate. Percival was dragging his opponent's body about, hither and thither over the meadow using this extraordinary method to divest the knight of his black armour! . . .

To the very end of his days, Sir Kay was not able to unravel the mystery of how the youth had triumphed over the knight, but when he reported the news of what he had just seen, the Queen laughed heartily for the first time that day.

She waited in vain for Percival to return to the Castle, but he — complete with armour and saddle — had ridden into the forest looking for King Arthur . . .

In the meantime, how was Sir Geraint faring? At first he followed the tracks through the forest and then, a few hours later, he rode out onto an open plain from where he could see, in the distance, a city and a castle. And, just at that moment, a man and a lady on horses passed through the city gate and a dwarf trudged after them.

"They must be my quarry," said Geraint to himself, and spurred his horse on. "I shall borrow some armour in the city, and then they will see what it means to offend the Queen," he mused.

Once in the city streets, he was astonished to see that it, and its inhabitants, were quite unknown to him. Above the settlement around the castle, he saw an entirely derelict

haired old man appeared before him and said, "Welcome, Sir Knight. If you are looking for shelter, we shall be glad to offer it to you." And he led Geraint into the house, where there was a small fire in a half-empty grate, beside which two ladies sat, embroidering.

"I am Earl Yniol, and this is my wife and my daughter Enid," said the old man, introducing his family to Sir Geraint and, as if he saw the question in Geraint's eyes, he added, "Yes, we are very poor now, and later I will explain to you why. But what has brought you to our city?"

Sir Geraint explained, and finished by saying, "I promised the Queen that I would punish the knight for the dwarf's rudeness. Would you be willing to lend me some armour and a weapon?"

"Perhaps my own armour will still be of some use to you," answered the Earl. "But first listen. That knight is a vicious man and he is my nephew. Until recently I looked after him as if he were my own, for he had no father or mother. I managed his lands and waited for him to come of age, when he would look after them himself. But he has always been disobedient, wild and rude, and he thought I was trying to deprive him of his estate. So he joined up with a band of robber-barons and, two years ago, he not only took what belonged to him, but he also drove me out of my own castle. That is

manor-house. "There is probably no one living there now, so I can have a rest," was the thought that struck Sir Geraint, as he rode through the open gate into the courtyard.

But when he dismounted, a white-it, towering above the city. He always needs money for revels with his friends; that is why he oppresses people and reduces them to poverty."

"And is there no one to stop him?" asked Sir Geraint.

The Earl shook his head sadly. "He is a good fighter," he said. "Once a year he holds a tournament and every time he wins. The main prize is a falcon, and so he calls himself the Knight of the Falcon."

"When is the next tournament to be held?" inquired Geraint, and the Earl replied, "Very soon now, yes, in fact it is tomorrow! But everyone who wishes to take part must bring with him a high-born maiden to whom he has pledged his heart."

The Earl fell silent, Geraint watched Enid out of the corner of his eye and, when he saw her smiling, he said, "My heart belongs to nobody yet; so, if you do not mind, I should like to ask your lovely daughter to render me that service."

Hearing this Enid blushed, but she still smiled at the Knight. The old Earl looked at the two young people, and agreed.

The next morning the Earl gave Sir Geraint his old armour. But alas! It was so rusty that all their efforts to clean it were in vain. Time was short, and

Geraint had to put on the armour in its rusty state. Enid had only a ragged and faded robe to wear and so, when they came riding to the meadow where the jousting was already in full swing, they looked like wandering players pretending to be a real knight and his lady. Indeed, all the spectators burst into unbridled laughter.

However, Geraint ignored the laughter and made for the jousting place. There, a solitary knight was riding to and fro. Others were lying on the ground or staggering away, but no one seemed keen to carry on the fight.

Thus it was Yniol's nephew who was to become victor again, and he had already directed his horse to the wooden pavilion to receive the falcon from the hands of his lady.

"Wait," shouted Sir Geraint. "You still have me to overthrow!" Enid handed him his first lance and he spurred his dapple-grey horse as the spectators laughed even more.

Then the two knights charged. At the very first thrust, both broke their lances. They each took a second and charged again. There was still no victor.

When Geraint rode towards Enid for the third time, she whispered to him, "This is my father's best weapon. Do not forget you are defending the Queen's honour!"

It was as if those words had given the Knight incredible power. With a single thrust, Geraint threw his op-

ponent out of the saddle and sent his helmet rolling to the ground. He lay on his back powerless; Geraint aimed the point of his spear at his foe's unprotected throat and said, "If you want to stay alive, apologize to the Queen for the rudeness of your dwarf! And, return your uncle's castle and lands to him! . . . Will you promise?"

"Yes, I will," gasped the knight in terror, gazing at the sinister rusty point of the lance, and only then was he allowed to rise. Sir Geraint rode past the now silent spectators to the pavilion to receive the falcon prize.

Of course, the Earl and his daughter rejoiced the most at Geraint's triumph. But even the defeated nephew came to realize that he had deserved to be taught a lesson and he sought to put right his previous misdeeds.

The Earl returned to his castle, and his nephew, in Geraint's company, set out for Camelot to present his apologies to the Queen. Nor were they alone — Sir Geraint took with him Enid, as his future bride.

At that time King Arthur and his huntsmen happened to be coming back from the hunt. They had tracked down the White Stag and were triumphantly bringing home its giant antlers. Then, they came upon Sir Kay. The Seneschal was so burning with impatience that he rushed to meet Arthur half way. He told the King all that had happened in the Castle and how the foolish Percival, who had probably never before seen a knight in armour in his life, had triumphed over the Black Knight.

The King was amazed. Then Sir Geraint with Enid and her cousin appeared on the scene, and confirmed one part of the Seneschal's story at least. They all went on their way to Camelot together. Everyone was talking and joking and the King kept asking about Percival, and where he might be.

As they came riding below a bare hill, they saw a horseman on its very top, and Sir Kay declared, "That is sure to be Percival. He has already put on the black armour of his defeated rival, and that dapple-grey nag of his could be recognized miles away!"

"So ride and fetch him!" commanded the King. And the Seneschal obediently spurred his horse up the hillside.

He called from a distance but Percival sat motionless, like a statue.

"Are you deaf?" cried Sir Kay, as he drew level.

"I am thinking," answered Percival, without as much as turning his head.

The Seneschal was furious. "Just be careful that too much thinking does not bring you down to the ground!" he scoffed. And he pushed Percival so hard that he only just managed to keep in the saddle. But, no sooner had he recovered his balance, than he smote Sir Kay's arm in return.

"Alas! You have broken my arm!"

159

moaned the Seneschal as he writhed with pain. But Percival was already on his way to meet the Knights of the Round Table who were watching everything in amazement.

Arthur himself asked incredulously, "Don't you know what strength you have? Sir Kay's arm may well be broken!"

"I do not," Percival confessed contritely. "That was the first blow I have ever dealt anyone in my life. I had never even seen a knight until recently." He continued, "My mother entrusted me to a hermit in the forest to bring me up. She did not want me to end up like my six brothers. They all fell in battles and tournaments . . . but I want to become a knight, even so. Therefore I have taken the hermit's advice, and have come to you."

"I think you are not far from becoming a knight. You are a very strong young man. And Sir Kay has had, once again, to pay the price of being so haughty," laughed King Arthur. Then he rode by Percival's side all the way to Camelot, asking questions about a hermit's life.

Percival stayed on at the Castle and, at Pentecost, became one of the Knights of the Round Table. Whereas Sir Geraint, with Enid, left for his estates in Devonshire, and the Queen herself gave them the fine antlers of the White Stag as a parting gift.

However, the first to leave Camelot was the ex-Falcon Knight. Guinevere accepted his apology and he was glad to have got out of the whole predicament unscathed, except with regard to his pride and pocket!

TALE FIFTEEN . . . KILHWCH AND OLWEN . . .

How Kilhwch comes to Camelot and makes a request. What the shepherd tells the Knights, and the tasks Kilhwch receives from Olwen's father. Sir Kay's adventure with Gwernach the Giant; Sir Gwrhyr's quest for Mabon the Huntsman; the ants help with the flax. Arthur and his Knights fulfil the last of the tasks, and what happens in the end.

The fame of the Knights of the Round Table ran throughout Arthur's realm and even spread to lands overseas. Many a man, whether high-born or of humble birth, came to Camelot seeking help or protection.

One day a young nobleman arrived, who was a sight to behold. His grey horse cantered as lightly as the morning mist and without bending a single leaf of grass. A pair of greyhounds with ruby-set collars, constantly circled their master. Silver spears and a gold-inlaid sword hilt glistened from under his purple mantle.

The steed carried the horseman right into the banqueting hall and, as each of those seated at the Round Table feasted their eyes on the young man, King Arthur said, "Be welcome and take a seat amongst us. But first tell us why you are in such a hurry that you have not even stabled your horse."

The young man, as if suddenly aware of his discourtesy, slid down from the saddle and knelt before Arthur. "I am Kilhwch, son of Kilydd, and my mother Goleuddydd was Prince Anlawdd's daughter," he said softly, pronouncing his own name rather like "Keelhookh".

"Then you are my cousin," said Arthur with a smile. "Tell me without fear what your request is — as long as you do not ask for Excalibur, Queen Guinevere or my ship *Prydwen!*"

The young man rose and said, "I will take cropping as a token of kinship."

The King had a golden comb and a pair of scissors with silver handles brought in, and performed the hair-cutting rite himself, according to custom. Then Kilhwch, without waiting to be urged, told his story.

"When my mother died, my father married again and my stepmother decided that I should marry Olwen, daughter of Ysbaddaden, the Chief Giant," he said. "Since the moment she spoke the maiden's name I have thought of none other. But so far I have looked for her in vain. So I have come here to ask your help."

Everyone at the Round Table had listened to Kilhwch in silence, but now a great many voices rose in the banqueting hall. They asked one another about Olwen and her father, but none had ever before heard their names mentioned, and no one could

think where they might be found.

The King, therefore, decided to organize a quest, and to take part in it himself. Curiously enough, the Knights he took along were not so much renowned for their prowess in fighting, but they possessed other qualities equally valuable, as it turned out.

Sir Gwrhyr Gwalstat had mastered all the languages spoken in the world, and even understood what the animals were saying. Sir Kyndelig never lost his way and so was able to act as a guide on the quest. Likewise Sir Kay — though he had not distinguished himself recently in any spectacular way—had not only the gift of remaining without sleep for as much as nine days, but he also knew how to hold his breath for very long periods. And when the King chose Sir Kay, he could not omit Sir Bedivere, the trusty friend who accompanied Sir Kay wherever the Seneschal went. The last choice fell on Sir Gawain, who just had to share in every adventure. Together with Kilhwch, they were, thus, a goodly number.

They set forth and, with Sir Kyndelig as their guide, arrived at a wide open plain where a mighty castle loomed in the distance. It was evening, however, before they gained the shelter of the high walls and under them a shepherd was tending his sheep.

They asked him, "Whose castle is this and whose sheep are you grazing?"

"I can see you do not come from these parts, otherwise you would never have ventured here," the man answered. "Everything all around belongs to the formidable Ysbaddaden." He then added, "Where have you come from?"

"From as far as Camelot; we are the Knights of the Round Table and are looking for the Giant's daughter, Olwen," said King Arthur.

But the shepherd cut him short anxiously. "Hush, you had better come to my cottage lest some misfortune befall you. And my wife is sure to know much more."

When they reached the shepherd's humble abode they learnt the horrible truth. Twenty-three of the shepherd's sons had been killed by Ysbaddaden and the youngest, named Goreu, was being kept hidden in a cupboard by his terrified mother. However, the presence of the Knights of the Round Table gave Goreu the courage to crawl out from his hiding place. He was a well-built brawny fellow and Sir Kay declared to his mother, "Why are you fearful for such a strong young man? Just let him come with us; I will personally guarantee that no one will harm a hair on his head, unless he kills me first."

They then asked about Olwen. They, and particularly Kilhwch, were delighted to hear that the maiden came to the shepherd's cottage every week, and they decided to await her there.

It was only a few days later, on a Saturday, that Olwen came to the cottage. She wore a silk gown of a flame colour, and her snow-white throat was adorned with a gold necklace set with emeralds and rubies. Her hair was fairer than the flowers of the common broom and her cheeks were rosier than a briar-rose. Such was her purity, that white clover grew in her footprints wherever she walked, and so she was rightly called Olwen of The White Track.

She caught sight of Kilhwch the moment she stepped over the threshold. As if she had known him for years and years, she sat down on the bench beside him. "I know we are predestined for each other; maybe since birth," she said. "But my father will not hear of me marrying. He is going to set you many very difficult tasks when you come to claim me, and there is only one piece of advice that I can give you. Promise that you will complete every single one of the tasks, otherwise we shall never be husband and wife, and you will lose your life."

With these words, Olwen rose from the bench and walked slowly back to the castle. Enchanted, Kilhwch watched as white sprays of clover sprang up in her footprints.

He did not even suspect that Olwen was followed, swiftly, by King Arthur's Knights. To gain entry to the castle, they had to fight and overcome nine guardsmen and kill nine watchdogs. It was only after Sir Gawain, his bare sword still in his hand, had returned and given him a brief account of what had happened, that Kilhwch girded himself with his sword and made for the castle. A moment later he appeared before Ysbaddaden, himself.

"So you want my daughter to be your wife," said the cruel old Giant angrily and, but for the Knights who surrounded Kilhwch, he might well have been attacked, there and then. Ysbaddaden went on mockingly, "Do not cherish any great hopes! I shall set you a number of difficult tasks. If you cope with them, you will win Olwen's hand; if not, it will be your death!"

"What you find difficult, I shall

find easy," answered Kilhwch, nothing daunted, but the Giant did not seem to be listening.

Using his fingers to lift his over-hanging eyebrows so as to see the young man better, he said, "While coming to the castle you must have noticed the red fields lying waste. I had flax sown there—nine bushels of the seed. Your first task will be to pick the seed to the very last, sow it in some other place, and gather in the flax. We shall then have something from which to weave Olwen's wedding veil."

"That is indeed a trifling task," laughed Kilhwch, but Ysbaddaden interrupted him. "Even if you do cope with that, there is the second task to fulfil," he said. "You must find Mabon the Huntsman who was lost when he was just three days old."

"I shall find Mabon with equal ease," said Kilhwch.

"Next you must seek two cubs of the She-Wolf, Gast Rhymhi. But you must bring them here, leading them on a leash woven from the hair of Dillus the Robber, otherwise they will escape," ordered the Giant.

"Even that will be quite easy, though it may seem difficult to you," observed Kilhwch.

Ysbaddaden looked at him in hatred and raised his voice till he was almost shouting. "Finally, you must get me

166

the sword of Gwernach the Giant! And, do not forget that only if you fulfil all the tasks, can Olwen be yours. Otherwise you forfeit your life!"

"I shall do everything as soon as possible," said Kilhwch, unafraid, "and then I shall take away your daughter." And he and the other Knights left the castle.

King Arthur took it upon himself to distribute the tasks amongst his Knights . . .

The first to set out was Sir Kay, charged with fetching the sword of Gwernach the Giant. Long was his quest, but finally he found himself in the huge castle which was Gwernach's seat.

The guard at the gate called on Sir Kay to stop and asked him, "Have you come to see Gwernach the Giant? Well, he doesn't receive people unless they have some extraordinary knowledge or skill!"

"And that I have, indeed," Kay answered. "Go and tell your master that I am the best sword grinder in the world."

And so, but a few moments later, Sir Kay was grinding the Giant's sword, with the sparks merrily flying away. Hardly two hours had passed before the blade was shining with a bluish light. The Giant was delighted and he put the weapon into his scabbard.

But Sir Kay's face immediately darkened. "What is that? What are you putting such a fine sword into?" he asked. "It is the most hideous scabbard I have ever seen!" Holding out his hand he went on, "Give it to me. I shall put that into good trim, also."

Unsuspecting, Gwernach returned the weapon to him. Sir Kay turned his back and pretended to inspect the scabbard. Suddenly, he faced the Giant, holding the bare sword with both hands. He raised it high and smote

taking the booty with him, he quickly made his way back to King Arthur.

Thus, Sir Kay had fulfilled his task with relative ease. But Sir Gwrhyr fared much worse. His assignment was to find Mabon the Huntsman, but wherever he went, no one could advise him. Finally, he thought to himself, "Since I have had no luck with men, I will ask the animals. After all, I do understand their language."

So he set out to find the Blackbird of Kilgwri, who was so old that the anvil upon which he wiped his bill every evening was now no bigger than a nut.

The Blackbird said, "I have never heard of Mabon in all my life. But there are other animals who have lived in the world longer than I have. Go and find the Stag of Redynvre. He may be able to help you."

Sir Gwrhyr set out in quest of the Stag and, finding him, asked for his help. The Stag fell thinking a while, then said, "Do you see that big tree-stump? I remember it when it was a slender oak. Then it grew into a tree with a hundred branches, and for a great many years now it has been only a rotting stump. Such is the time I have lived here. But of Mabon the Huntsman I have no knowledge at all. Perhaps the Eagle of Gwernabwy might help you?" And the Stag led Sir Gwrhyr under a high rock upon which the Eagle was sitting.

But not even the Eagle was able to answer the query, and all he could do

Gwernach powerfully. The Giant fell like a blasted oak.

Sir Kay then helped himself from the vast treasures of the castle and, was to give advice. "I no longer remember how long it has been since, one evening, I started pecking at the stars," he said. "Yet I know nothing about Mabon. Nor is there anyone left who could tell you about him, except, perhaps, the Salmon of Llyn Llyw. Go and try him!"

Sir Gwrhyr followed the Eagle's advice and went down to the river where the Salmon lived. After a while of waiting, the enormous fish stuck his head out of the water and Sir Gwrhyr said to him, "No man or animal knows where I might find Mabon the Huntsman, son of Modron. You are my one and only hope."

"Mabon sits in a deep dungeon in Gloucester. I have heard his lamenta-tions in the water," said the Salmon, solemnly. "But he cannot be set free without a fight. That is the message you should give to the King, from me."

With the greatest speed Sir Gwrhyr returned to King Arthur, who quickly gathered his army to attack Gloucester. And while the bloody battle for the city was raging, Sir Kay and Sir Bedivere sat on the Salmon's back, and it was with his help that they got to the prison wall which was set deep in the water.

The Salmon submerged and Sir Kay, still on its back, held his breath until he had broken through the wall and set Mabon the Huntsman free. Then, together with the King, they re-

turned to the shepherd's cottage. Only Sir Gwrhyr rode back all alone. On his way he listened to the talking of both men and beasts. Then, all of a sudden, he heard a heart-breaking lament and someone called, "Help! Somebody please help us, or we shall all burn to death!"

Sir Gwrhyr looked in the direction of the cry and saw smoke pouring from a heap on the ground.

He ran closer and saw a big ant-hill enclosed by fire on all sides. The ants were running to and fro, but they could no longer find even a tiny gap between the flames through which they might escape.

So Sir Gwrhyr drew his sword and used the flat blade to put out the fire.

"Thank you for saving us," cried the ants. "Is there anything that we can do to help you, in return?"

The knight smiled, and was about to continue his journey when he remembered the first task that had been assigned to Kilhwch. He said to the ants, "Yes, you can help me! Bring me the nine bushels of flax seed that Ysbaddaden had sown in the red fields near his castle!"

This the ants readily agreed to do, and Sir Gwrhyr continued on his way to the shepherd's cottage. When he arrived, the ants had got through half their work. And before dusk fell, one of them, who walked with a limp, brought in the very last seed for full measure.

The next day, Kilhwch sowed all the nine bushels in a new place, and before long the first shoots appeared.

Now there was only one of the tasks left to do. This was to bring in the young of the She-Wolf, Gast Rhymhi, on a leash woven from the hair of Dillus the Robber.

Arthur knew that the She-Wolf lived in a far-away cave by the sea, and set forth, alone, aboard his ship, the *Prydwen*, in quest of the wolf-cubs. At the same time, however, he sent Sir Kay and Sir Bedivere in search of the Robber, so that they could obtain the hair for the leash.

The Robber dwelt in a deep forest and boar's meat was his favourite delicacy. This the Seneschal knew very well, and so he had several boars killed, and then he placed them in a suitable spot, ready to set a trap for Dillus.

Hardly an hour had passed before the Robber found the meat. He made a big fire and started to cook it. The whole forest was filled with the smell of roast boar.

Then Dillus set about his feast. One boar, he ate at a sitting. He considered whether he should roast another one, but the feasting had made him tired, so he lay down and slept, snoring till the trees shook at their roots.

That was the moment Sir Kay and Sir Bedivere were waiting for. They did not want to kill the Robber—the leash would break if they did. Instead, they

just cut off his beard while he slept, and then stole out of the forest unobserved.

Sir Kay wove the beard into a strong rope and gave it to King Arthur, when he returned — after many adventures — with the wolf-cubs.

Thus with the help of the Knights of the Round Table, Kilhwch fulfilled the tasks he had been set. With all the trophies gained, he went into the castle to claim Olwen. The shepherd's son, Goreu, was the only man to accompany him.

Kilhwch presented Ysbaddaden with the sword of Gwernach the Giant, and brought before him Mabon the Huntsman and the two wolf-cubs on a leash made from the Robber's hair. Then, he stepped to the window and showed the Giant the sprouting flax, and asked, "Will you give me your daughter now?"

"Yes, I will," Ysbaddaden nodded his approval. "But it is King Arthur and his Knights whom you have to thank for everything. By yourself, you would never have fulfilled the tasks,

171

nor would I ever have entrusted Olwen to your care."

At that moment Olwen came into the hall, and when she saw what had been achieved, she was delighted. Soon after, she left with Kilhwch and they travelled to his estates.

However, while for the two of them this day was a happy one above all others, for the cruel old Giant it became his last. Goreu, the shepherd's son, was not prepared to leave the deaths of his twenty-three brothers unavenged, and he killed Ysbaddaden with one mighty blow from Gwernach's huge sword.

TALE SIXTEEN . . .
SIR GALAHAD;
THE HOLY GRAIL;
SIR PELLEAS
AND ETTARD . . .

On campaigns and festivals held by King Arthur. Sir Lancelot knights Galahad and the Siege Perilous becomes occupied. The Holy Grail appears briefly, and the Knights of the Round Table set out in quest of it. The sad story of Sir Pelleas and the heartless maiden Ettard, and how Sir Gawain forgets his vow. The strange utterance of Sir Mordred.

Years passed like water under a bridge, and the Knights of the Round Table lived on. Order and peace prevailed in Britain, but in Ireland a man named Gilmarius rose up against Arthur. So the King had a large navy built and, with the help of his faithful, defeated Gilmarius' armies.

Not long after this, the Orkney Islanders refused to obey Sir Gawain, who had inherited the rule of the Orkneys from Lot, his father. There, too, Arthur's Knights were victorious. Then, they had to sail to Norway and after that, to other far lands.

Their renown in battle was growing. Noblemen in their hundreds came streaming to Camelot to pay tribute to Arthur, and the King prepared great and spectacular festivities to honour his guests. At these, all enjoyed themselves. For days they could listen to sweet music and song, eat their fill of choice dainties, drink rare wines and, last but not least, take part in the many games and jousts.

Not only were there tournaments and battles between the knights, but also archery, javelin throwing and contests in the casting of heavy stones. Some, less active visitors, preferred a game of dice, or chess.

From the galleries, gentle damsels and ladies urged on the knights who were wearing their coats-of-arms.

The festivities went on for three days and King Arthur rewarded each victor with a precious gift. Then, on the fourth day, he called together the men-at-arms who had rendered him the most faithful service in the past, and rewarded them with titles to land and even a town or castle.

However, the time was near when few Knights would be seated at the Round Table . . .

One day, Sir Gawain was riding and it chanced that he found himself near the cave where Merlin was imprisoned.

The Knight had little hope that the old man could still be alive. Thus, he was greatly astonished when he heard Merlin's voice. "Stop for a while, Sir Gawain, and listen to what I have to say to you!"

Gawain's horse, Gringolet, stiffened as if rooted to the ground, and Merlin went on, "Hasten to Camelot! The Holy Grail is leaving us, and it is time to proclaim a great quest for it!"

That was all Merlin said and, though Sir Gawain kept urging him to explain what he meant, the cave remained silent as the grave.

It is important that we realize the importance of the Holy Grail. This was the cup used by Jesus at the Last Supper and in which Joseph of Arimathea received the Saviour's blood at the Cross. It symbolized absolute Christian purity, as Sir Gawain would have known well.

However, there was nothing he could do but return to Camelot, where he found preparations had been made for the celebration of Pentecost. Many with familiar faces were present, such as Sir Lancelot and Sir Kay, as well as some new and dreaded fighters, including Sir Percival.

However, Sir Gawain had no time to convey Merlin's message to all the Knights of the Round Table; for suddenly an unknown fair damsel on a little white horse entered the hall, and said, "I have come from King Pelles and beg Sir Lancelot to follow me, immediately."

"I will gladly oblige the King, whatever his wish," replied the Knight.

Then Queen Guinevere spoke. "It is not right, Sir Knight, that you should leave us, just at Pentecost. Particularly when you know nothing about what you are heading for."

"He will be back with you tomorrow, by dinner time, noble Queen," pledged the damsel.

174

That settled the matter. Lancelot ordered his squire to prepare his steed and armour, and before long he was on his way with the damsel.

They rode through the forest for several hours before coming to an open glade. There, the snow-white walls of an abbey rose to the sky. To Sir Lancelot's surprise, who should be in the abbey but his cousin Sir Bors, son of King Bors, who — as we know — had helped Arthur in the battle of Bedegraine.

No sooner had the two fallen into each other's arms than the abbess came in, bringing with her a young man. He was, in fact, still a lad and was the very image of Sir Lancelot. Yes, indeed, it was none other than Galahad, Sir Lancelot's own son!

Sir Lancelot caught his breath in elation and pride. After a while, he asked his son if there was anything for which he wished.

"I am fifteen years of age, and my one wish is for you to make me a knight, for as I hear from King Pelles, my grandfather, you are the best fighter of the Round Table," replied Galahad, gravely.

Sir Lancelot was only too happy to comply with his son's request and, having learnt from him that they were to meet again soon, the two bade each other farewell. Then, next morning, Lancelot and Sir Bors departed for Camelot.

When they appeared in the ban-

queting hall just before dinner, the Knights of the Round Table were delighted at Lancelot's punctual return — Queen Guinevere most of all.

They all took their seats, and at that moment King Arthur realized that every seat in the circle, except of course for the Siege Perilous, was filled.

However, Sir Kay recalled yet another matter. "It is the custom that, before we go to our meat on holy days, we hear of some new adventure. So perhaps someone today may tell a story that we haven't heard before?"

Sir Lancelot was on the point of recounting what had made him ride away from Camelot in such a hurry the day before, when in came a very old man dressed in white, leading by the hand a very young knight clad in dark red armour.

To his amazement Lancelot recognized the boy to be his own son, Galahad, but by then the old man had stepped to the Siege Perilous and said, "This is your siege, sir."

The young man sat himself down in a carefree manner. No evil befell him and, in an instant, the inscription 'THIS IS THE SIEGE PERILOUS' vanished and, in golden letters, appeared the words, 'THIS IS THE SIEGE OF SIR GALAHAD THE HOLY KNIGHT'.

By then everyone had noticed how like Sir Lancelot the young man was in appearance, and many tongues were wagging, hinting that, by his deeds, he was certain to exceed the glory of his father.

When dinner was ended King Arthur, according to custom, held a tournament in the green field under the Castle. In this contest, Sir Galahad showed his prowess, even though he had no shield, and would not hear of borrowing one. Finally, only he, his father and Sir Percival remained in the saddle with their lances unbroken. These three then fought on, but still

with no final result. King Arthur thus put an end to the jousting and adjudged victory to all three, without distinction.

There was to be no end to the marvels that day. After Vespers, when they were seated again about the Round Table and waiting for supper

to be brought in, there was a mighty crash of thunder, as though the whole Castle were tumbling down.

The gloom of the great hall was cut by the flame of dazzling rays. Above the Round Table was a cloth of white samite which covered a golden cup, so that none could see it. At the same

179

time the air was filled with an intoxicating spicy fragrance and the Table all but sagged under the weight of so much meat and drink as appeared before the Knights.

Then, the veiled golden cup began to float away, as if borne by an invisible bird, and then it vanished altogether.

For a long time not a sound was to be heard, then Sir Galahad spoke, with reverence. "That which we have just beheld, is the most precious object in all the world. It is the Holy Grail! Only he who is clean of all his sins can ever achieve it."

When he heard Galahad's words Sir Gawain recalled Merlin's prophecy and declared, "It was the Holy Grail, and it is leaving us. I know, too, that unless we regain it, it will mean the end of the Round Table and of our brotherhood. Therefore I take this vow: I will set out in quest of the Holy Grail on the morrow, and not come back before a year and a day have passed . . ."

After Sir Gawain's words, all the other Knights rose and vowed likewise. This was to be the one and only occasion that all the one hundred and fifty sieges of the Round Table were filled.

In vain Arthur tried to persuade them all not to go away, arguing that they would never again come together and in vain did the Queen and her ladies-in-waiting, who loved the Knights, shed sad tears . . .

Early next morning, the Knights of the Round Table set out from Camelot on their quest for the Holy Grail. Before long the Castle and the town were left behind and, as agreed, each set off along a different road according to his own choice. The Knights were to find great adventure for the next year — but that is another story. We shall remain, for the time being, at Camelot to find out how the days passed there . . .

King Arthur, with all his Knights absent, was obliged to gather together a new company of knights, and so he proclaimed a great tournament. Messengers rode out to the remotest corners of Britain and left notices written on parchment at every castle, citadel and cross-roads.

The tidings reached Sir Pelleas of the Islands, so called because he lived on one of a remote group of small islands. He was a good fighter and had taught himself to wield arms although, on his island, he had no chance of testing his skill against others. The island was inhabited only by fishermen, and Pelleas never ventured far away.

However, he now thought that he would try his luck at the Royal Court, and had himself taken by fishing boat to the English shore, continuing his journey on horseback.

Since he had never in his life seen anything but the island and his own town, he admired everything he came upon—the wide forests as well as the trees themselves, the multitude of

game and birds and, above all, the
distant castles and settlements.

Then something happened to make
him very discomfited. His horse was
wading up to its breast through the
high bracken when, suddenly the
knight saw several damsels on horseback. The beautiful leader of them
asked him with a smile, "Please, Sir,
how shall we get to Camelot?"

Dazzled by her beauty, the knight
could hardly answer. At home he was
accustomed to seeing rough fisher-
women dressed in shabby rags who

The damsel's smile became a ringing laugh. She started back and the other damsels burst out laughing with her. Sir Pelleas remained bemused and all that he managed to bring out, in his agitation, was, "I am also on my way to Camelot to take part in a tournament. For you I shall triumph. For it is you and no one else I shall love as long as I live!"

However, the damsel only laughed again, even louder than before, and before Pelleas could do anything to stop her, she and her retinue had disappeared in the bracken.

As though in a dream the knight continued to Camelot. He sat at the banquet held by King Arthur before the tournament, entirely distracted. The only thing he had discovered was that the damsel's name was Ettard, and that she lived not far from the spot where they had met.

When the jousting took place, Pelleas held the field all the time, and deservedly received a sword from King Arthur and a gold coronet from Queen Guinevere.

He immediately approached Ettard, who was sitting beside the Queen, and set the coronet on her head. "Never shall I fight for other colours than yours, nor shall I ever love any other maiden but yourself," he declared passionately.

But the damsel rebuffed him again. "So, you have found your tongue at last. But the fact is, I do not care

constantly croaked like crows. But this damsel was clad in samite and silk and her voice recalled the music of a harp. Her face was so sweet and soft that, instead of answering, Pelleas reached out to touch her.

a straw for you, even if that should bring you to death through grief!"

Her answer made the knight very unhappy. However, he resolved to follow the damsel come what may, and always to remain close to her.

The Queen and the other noble ladies were scandalized by Ettard's behaviour. "It is not right to despise the love of such a fine knight," said Guinevere. "Other ladies, some far lovelier than yourself, would esteem Sir Pelleas' affection if he should show it to them."

"What is so fine about him? If the Knights of the Round Table had not gone in quest of the Holy Grail, that nitwit would not have won! Sir Lance-

lot might have become victor, and such a man I would never spurn!" retorted the maiden spitefully and she left the gallery angrily.

She and her retinue left Camelot early. She did not realize that Sir Pelleas was secretly following her, and it was only when she was approaching her castle that he caught up with her and begged her again to be kinder to him.

However, Ettard called her men-at-arms from the castle. Hardly anyone would have held his own against such odds, but Pelleas routed them all until they, and Ettard with them, were forced to seek refuge behind the strong castle walls.

183

Do you suppose that this finally persuaded the knight to stop pursuing Ettard? Nothing of the kind; he began to roam around the walls, without food or drink, just to be near her. Not even this, however, was enough to soften Ettard's heart. Week after week, she would send out her men-at-arms to fight Sir Pelleas, but he overthrew them all.

Once, he even let himself be bound hand and foot and shamefully conveyed to the castle under a horse's belly. But once again the cruel damsel spurned and mocked him as she would a mangy dog.

Poor Pelleas was really at his wits'

end. Then, one day he saw a knight on horseback, beneath the castle. It was Sir Gawain astride Gringolet, on his quest for the Holy Grail. The sight of the tortured face of the unknown man made him halt, and he listened to the story Sir Pelleas had to tell.

The young man begged Sir Gawain to intercede with Ettard on his behalf.

"But how?" asked Sir Gawain. "I will gladly promise to do anything I can to move her heart . . ."

"There is nothing left but to find out whether she will feel sorry if I perish," said Sir Pelleas. "So take my armour and tell her you have killed me. Then you will see what can be done."

Sir Gawain agreed and pledged his word as a knight that he would fulfil anything asked of him. Then they exchanged armour and shields, and Gawain knocked at the castle gate.

After a while Ettard's voice was heard saying, "What do you want all the time? Isn't it enough that I had you thrown out like a dog?"

"I am not who you think I am," answered Sir Gawain, lifting his visor.

Immediately, the gate opened and the knight rode into the courtyard as Pelleas just watched sadly from his hiding place. Sir Gawain dismounted and gave his name, and the damsel conducted him to the castle.

Later, he told her the invented story that he had killed Pelleas in a duel and had taken his armour. Ettard flung back her head till her dark hair flowed in streams over her shoulders and said, "If it were someone else, I might feel sorry for him, just because he had once been a good fighter. But as for Pelleas, I can only wish him the end he met with, because he was over-persistent." Then Ettard gave Gawain a bright smile and added, "And I will do anything to please you!"

At once she commanded that silk tents should be put up in the court-yard, barrels of rare wine brought, and a fire made for roasting venison. Mean-while, the musicians had tuned their instruments, and when the entertain-ment began, Sir Gawain forgot all about his promise to Sir Pelleas.

It was a warm May evening and the air was filled with a hundred intoxi-cating sweet scents. As the moon ascended in the night sky, and with the increasing number of draughts of vintage wine, Sir Gawain, who was fickle in his affections, was seized with love for the beautiful Ettard, and she did not discourage him . . .

In the meantime, Pelleas was wait-ing under the walls of the castle, as arranged. The night passed, another came and went, and a third followed. When even that had passed, the knight put on his armour and, with the fear in his heart that Sir Gawain had met with misfortune, he made for the gate.

Unobserved he passed into the courtyard and walked towards the three silk tents. Sword in hand he looked into the nearest one, but there were only a few drunken men-at-arms sleeping there. Nor did he pause long at the second tent, for inside he just saw four noble damsels asleep on four beds.

However, at the third tent he stopped. Inside were Ettard and Sir Gawain, in each other's arms.

At once the torment Sir Pelleas had endured turned into hatred for the knight. He lifted his sword to kill Sir Gawain but, at the last moment, he held back.

Instead, he laid the bare blade of his sword—the one he had received from King Arthur for his triumph in the tournament — across the throats of

185

Gawain and Ettard. Then he turned, mounted his horse, and left.

Maddened with sorrow and hatred from that day onward Sir Pelleas wandered about the countryside. Wherever he went, he poured out words of abuse upon Sir Gawain and, indeed, on all the Knights of the Round Table.

The first man to hear the slanderous tirade was Sir Mordred, Sir Gawain's brother—he with the foxy face. But, strange to tell, it never occurred to him to defend the good names of his brother and the other Knights. He just smiled to himself and muttered strangely, "Lo, a flash of lighting; my time has come! . . ."

TALE SEVENTEEN ...
SIR PERCIVAL AND
BLANCHEFLEUR;
LOHENGRIN AND
ELSA ...

Sir Gawain has a strange dream and when this is interpreted, he abandons his quest for the Holy Grail. Sir Percival's adventures; how he marries and leaves a son named Lohengrin, later to become known as the Knight with the Swan. Lohengrin's adventures in Brabant and his predestined departure.

When Sir Gawain and Ettard felt the cold blade of the sword at their throats, they were very afraid. The damsel fled into the castle with loud cries and the Knight thought that he would rather melt into thin air than experience such feelings of guilt and fear.

Therefore, he mounted Gringolet as quickly as possible and set forth again on his quest of the Holy Grail. Day and night he stayed in the saddle, not eating or sleeping. But all his efforts were of no avail. What is more, Sir Gawain met no one and encountered no adventure, and he felt more and more distressed.

The summer passed. Then, just at Michaelmas he came upon a ruined chapel. As he had grown very tired, he dismounted, let Gringolet loose to graze, and lay down in the shade of a spreading oak-tree. The branches

above him rustled softly and silvery threads of gossamer floated gently in the breeze. Soon the Knight fell asleep and, as he slept, he had a very strange dream.

He saw rich pasture land on which was a large herd of sturdy bulls. Sir Gawain counted as many as one hundred and fifty, and all of them but three were completely black. The remaining three bulls were of pure white. After a while the animals left the pasture, but later the Knight saw them again. This time they looked lean and sickly, and many less than the full number had returned . . .

So vivid was the dream that Sir Gawain awoke. Of the pasture and the bulls, there was not a trace anywhere. Only Gringolet was there, and he raised his head in surprise and pricked up his ears. The Knight called him and they set out on another journey. But Sir Gawain did not ride for long. Before evening he had reached a log cabin and in front of it was an old man in a long robe which reached down to the ground.

At long last Sir Gawain had come across a human being! He greeted the old man courteously, and when he learnt that the latter was a hermit, he told him of the dream.

The holy man listened to the

Knight in silence. Then he looked at him gravely and said, "This is indeed an extraordinary dream; you will want to know what it means . . . Well, the rich pasture land represents the Round Table, and the one hundred and fifty bulls are King Arthur's Knights. As these set out in quest of the Holy Grail, so the bulls left their pasture. However, only three knights will reach the Holy Grail — remember you saw but three pure white bulls in your dream."

"And shall I be among them?" asked Sir Gawain before the hermit could go on.

"You, like most of the others, will not succeed in your quest. You have not lived a good life and you have committed dishonourable deeds. You had better take my advice and return to Camelot!"

Sir Gawain bowed his head. "Who then will be the elect ones?" he asked.

"I could tell you that now, but you will come to know that yourself, in due time," replied the old man, whereupon he, and the hermitage with him, dissolved from view.

Without being urged, Gringolet started back to Camelot at a trot and, by nightfall, the guards were opening the gate of Arthur's Castle to let the Knight in.

Not long after Sir Gawain, other Knights of the Round Table began returning from their search for the Holy Grail. But there were many who

stil pursued the quest, Sir Lancelot amongst them.

He roamed the forests and mountains and at last embarked on a ship to a faraway country — unfortunately the ancient books do not give its name. He crossed and recrossed the land for some time until, eventually, he met Sir Percival.

"We can ride together," suggested Sir Percival. "Not far from here there lives a lady, a friend from my young

189

days whom I have not seen for many a year. She will, no doubt, be happy to receive us." Lancelot agreed and the horses of the two Knights fell into step, side by side.

Suddenly, however, a horseman rushed at them out of the thicket. He was hidden behind a huge white shield with a red cross emblazoned on it. Before they could move aside, he had flown past at such a speed that they both tumbled to the ground.

Sir Percival was injured by his fall, and so his companion was very

relieved when, soon after, they saw the castle they were seeking.

Percival's friend was called Blanchefleur, and she was so beautiful that even Sir Lancelot trembled at the sight of her. Nevertheless, he did not stay at the castle, for he had a suspicion that the knight who had rushed at them was his own son, Galahad.

However, let us leave Sir Lancelot as he continues his quest, and let us stay with the lovely Blanchefleur and Sir Percival. For it is here that the story of a very special knight has its begin-

190

nings. This knight would be the last to remind the world of the Round Table and the Holy Grail, when the original heroes were all sleeping their last sleep . . .

At the castle, Sir Percival rapidly recovered from his injury, thanks to the care and love with which Blanchefleur nursed him. No wonder then that he forgot all about his original mission and, a few weeks later, he and Blanchefleur married.

It seemed that Sir Percival had completely given up his quest for the Holy Grail. But then the unexpected happened! As he was sleeping, he saw in his dreams a golden cup filled with red blood, and that blood flowed down the sides of the cup, like bitter tears . . .

Sir Percival roused himself from his sleep. He dressed in silence and went to the stable, where he saddled his horse. Without a single word of farewell to his wife, he rode out into the darkness, once again in quest of the Holy Grail.

To begin with, Blanchefleur could not believe that her husband had abandoned her so cruelly. But when the weeks and months passed and Sir Percival still failed to return, she sought out a learned Moor, who had dwelt in the castle from time immemorial and was one of the wisest men in the world.

"I know why you have come to see me, my daughter; I have been expecting you for some time now," said the

old man in welcome, and he rose from his studies of a yellowing parchment. "It was by chance that Sir Percival came to our castle. And it was your

191

beauty and your love that made him forget, for a short time, the mission for which he is predestined," he said. "It was only after your marriage that he remembered it. That is why he has departed for ever."

"For ever?" The unhappy Blanchefleur would not believe the words. "And what kind of a mission is it, when it destroys our love?" she asked, tearfully.

"Sir Percival is one of the few Knights of the Round Table who will attain the Holy Grail. Do not wrong

him, however, by believing that he has forgotten you," answered the wise man. "You will bear him a son," he went on, "and that son will make amends to you for everything. That is all I can tell you, except for a warning. You should not reveal to your son the name of his father. When the time comes, he will learn that from me."

Blanchefleur's heart was less heavy when she left the wise man. And indeed, before long, she gave birth to a son and she called him Lohengrin. Fair-haired and blue-eyed, it seemed as if he was trying to compensate his mother for the love she found but lost so soon afterwards.

After a carefree childhood, the boy quickly learnt horse-riding, falconry, hunting and weaponry, but he also showed an unusual interest in the Arts. As for his mother, he loved her and worshipped her like a saint. When the time came for him to take part in knightly games and jousts, he fought for only Blanchefleur's colours—green and white — and he never toasted any-one but her. He did not want to marry, even though many of the noble maidens in the neighbourhood would have gladly accepted his wooing, and his mother herself often urged him to wed.

Blanchefleur did not live to see him married, however. One damp and cold Autumn she took to her bed, and before the oaks and beeches on the neighbouring hills dressed themselves again in Spring leaves, she died in her son's arms, reconciled with the world. With the last remnants of her ebbing strength, she told Lohengrin to ask the wise Moor about his father.

For a long time the sad youth did not think of this advice. Then, one day, he found himself in the palace library.

Just as, two decades before, when the unhappy Blachefleur had come there to seek advice, the old man sat

studying a yellowing parchment. At once he stepped forward and welcomed the visitor with these words: "I have been expecting you for several days now, dear Lohengrin, to tell you everything I know about your father. Come, sit down and listen . . ."

And then the wise man began to talk about the Knights of the Round Table and their quest of the Holy Grail. But chiefly he spoke about the adventures of Sir Percival, some of which we are yet to hear about, for they had occurred many years before Lohengrin came of age. Then the Moor finished his story by saying, "Your father was one of the few to attain the Holy Grail. But he is no long-

er alive, so it would be useless for you to search for him. But you, also, are destined to meet with great adventures in the wide world, and you will attain no less a glory." He continued, "But there is one thing you should be on your guard against. If you disclose your father's name to any person, you must part with that person — no matter how dear to you they may be . . ."

On that very day, Lohengrin had his grooms prepare his grey steed for a long journey. And, before dusk, Lohengrin had left his native castle.

We do not know for how long he journeyed, whether for weeks or months, but one day he reached a wide, raging river. Trees, bushes, and parts of its banks were being swept along by the river and the grey horse dared not enter the water.

Then, at just the right moment, a ferryman appeared with a heavy barge on which he could ferry several horsemen and their horses. Lohengrin was on the point of entering the barge when the ferryman stopped him. "You will find the boat destined for you a few miles downstream from here. My duty is to provide you with your armour," he said.

Lohengrin was surprised and delighted with his silver armour, which was dazzling to the sight. What particularly appealed to him was the wonderful helmet which featured a skilfully wrought swan. Then, he noticed that the barge and the ferryman had disappeared, as though the water had soundlessly closed over them.

So he rode along the river and, after an hour's ride, he saw another barge with another ferryman whose face was more furrowed than that of the first, and whose beard was even whiter. He said, "You will find your boat, Lohengrin, still a few miles further downstream. I have waited just to hand over these weapons to you." And the ferryman lifted out of the barge a sword with a diamond-set hilt, a lance and a heavy shield. On the shield, under the image of the swan, an inscription glittered: 'OPPOSE THE STRONG, PROTECT THE WEAK'.

Then the second ferryman and his barge vanished like the morning mist over the water.

Having girt himself with the sword, and fixed the shield to his saddle, Lohengrin set out along the river again. By a wide creek, he saw the greatest wonder of all: a boat made

195

of rare wood, inlaid and carved, and at its prow a large snow-white swan was leashed with a golden chain. The silent bird seemed to be inviting him, with its eyes, to embark.

There was enough room in the vessel for both Lohengrin and his grey. He looked for oars, but there were none. Then, suddenly, the swan spread its wings, which grew crimson in the late afternoon sun. Like an arrow the boat shot along the river surface behind the bird, then lifted high, and soon Lohengrin saw the two banks merge into a single greenish line. Where was the swan taking him? And why?

The river was the Scheldt, and far downstream was the city of Antwerp. This was the seat of the very young Duchess of Brabant and Limburg, whose name was Elsa. She was fair-haired and blue-eyed just as was Lohengrin, and her pure face shone with the beauty of a fresh Spring day. But, at the time of which we are speaking, she was tormented by fears and sorrow.

For it had happened that when Elsa's father, the old Duke of Brabant, was dying, he entrusted not only his estates, but also the guardianship of his youngest daughter, to his most faithful servant Telramund.

197

There is no denying that Telramund would not have hesitated to lay down his life for the Duke, but he could be vicious and cruel, and his wild face was always enough to make Elsa terrified of him.

No wonder then that she avoided him as much as she could and, when he assumed the rule over Brabant and began to woo her, she declared, "I would rather go into a nunnery!"

At that time Telramund only sneered, "And should I not marry a nun if she has your beautiful face?"

Since then he had continued to court Elsa so persistently that, if she did not remain in her chamber, she really did not know where to hide from him.

There was many a young man of noble family who had affection for the lovely and sweet Duchess of Brabant, but each of these was driven away by Telramund, or overthrown in a duel.

In the end, since Elsa still rejected him, Telramund brought his suit before Emperor Henry, himself.

Henry had known the old Duke of Brabant quite well, for the Duke had helped him more than once in his campaigns against the savage Huns. This was enough to make him favourably disposed towards the maiden. But he also knew Telramund, who was rendering the Empire no less necessary services. So after much heart-searching, the Emperor made a discreet decision in the Brabant cause.

The last word in the whole matter would be left to a test, to be held on a certain day. A large tournament field would be built beneath the city of Antwerp, on the banks of the River Scheldt. Finally, every three hours, heralds would sound their trumpets to call anyone prepared to challenge Telramund. Only he who triumphed over Telramund could alter Elsa's fate . . .

So they built the tournament field, and scaffoldings and galleries were constructed for hundreds, maybe even thousands of spectators. Even so, when the appointed day arrived and the heralds for the first time sounded their trumpets, there were still many onlookers for whom there was no room on the river bank.

While Telramund, on his powerful stately bay, stood motionless waiting for his first challenger, Elsa looked down from the pavilion, fearfully. However, no one appeared.

Three long hours passed and the heralds blew their trumpets for the second time. The sun was rising higher and higher in the sky when Telramund lifted the visor of his helmet and commanded his squires to fetch water for his horse. The bay gulped down the water and its master looked across towards the pavilion where Elsa, having abandoned all hope, wept.

199

The bells of St Mary's Cathedral and the other churches had just begun to ring out noon when the heralds blew their trumpets for the third time. And at that moment a strange sound came from the Scheldt. Among the boats, ferries and sailing ships pressed close to one another on the river, a huge white swan was clearing a path for itself. By a golden chain, it was hauling a vessel, in which stood an unknown knight clad in silver armour. Yes, it was no other than Lohengrin!

Telramund could not believe his eyes. As he wondered, Lohengrin came within the palisades and urged his grey steed towards his opponent.

"I do not wish to fight you to the death," he told Telramund in his calm clear voice. "Just give up Elsa; Brabant and Limburg you can keep."

"Do you believe I would put up with such a small reward?" shouted Telramund. "I want everything, or nothing!"

So, from the opposite ends of the tournament field, the two contestants charged at each other. Fierce was the impact of the spears into the shields but, while Telramund remained in the saddle, Lohengrin tumbled onto the grass. He quickly raised himself, ignoring the mocking cries of his opponent's followers: "Just like a swan's feather has he come down from the saddle," they jeered.

Then, Telramund bore down on Lohengrin again, spurring his bay on

whilst reining him in, in an attempt to make the horse trample Lohengrin to death.

Elsa's fearful cry was enough to chill the blood. But Telramund's horse saw the defenceless knight and, instead of trampling him, the horse collapsed backwards taking his rider with him.

Telramund had no chance to leave the saddle. Only his anguished death cry was heard before the weight of the horse's body broke his neck.

Thus, the fight was over and the young Duchess knew that she could now decide her own fate. Overcome with happiness she ran up to Lohengrin to thank him.

Everyone was delighted: Elsa, the Emperor Henry and the whole of Brabant with them. And to make that joy a lasting one, it soon began to be rumoured, both in Antwerp and in the countryside, that the Knight with the Swan was about to take the young Duchess as his wife.

This rumour was, in fact, true, but before the two came to stand before the altar, the maiden had to promise that she would never ask who he was, let alone who his father had been.

Thus it came about that Lohengrin stayed in Brabant and reigned over the Duchy like a wise and experienced ruler. Before long Elsa gave him two sons, and it seemed that their happiness could not be clouded by anything till the end of their days. And yet this was not to be . . .

The Emperor Henry would visit Brabant for pleasure and, as time went on, he would bring with him his own children. The boys played with Lohengrin's children; now and then they would squabble or even scuffle, but soon they would become friends again as children will. Then, one day, Elsa found her own sons in tears. They complained that the other boys had scoffed at them, saying that only God knew where their father had come from and telling them what low-born ancestors he must have had.

Angrily, the unhappy Duchess ran to Lohengrin and, forgetting her solemn pledge, asked him to explain everything truthfully.

The Knight with the Swan frowned deeply, but did not utter a word of objection. He sat the boys on his knee and told them everything that he had learnt about his own father, Percival, the Knights of the Round Table and their quest of the Holy Grail.

When he had finished his story, he looked sadly into Elsa's eyes and said, "You know what you promised. Since you have broken that promise, I must go away from here for ever. For that is what is written in the book of fate. It was revealed to me by the old and wise Moor."

And, despite the wailing of his wife and his sons, Lohengrin rose and walked slowly through the high grass to the River Scheldt.

There the great white swan with the golden chain was waiting for him and the familiar boat rocked on the water. Lohengrin embarked, then looked back and waved for the last time. Soon, all there was to be seen was the foaming water of the Scheldt as, above the river, the snow-white bird's wings disappeared into the vast distance . . .

TALE EIGHTEEN ...
THE QUEST
OF THE HOLY
GRAIL ...

Sir Lancelot finds Sir Galahad. How Sir Galahad obtains his shield. Sir Lancelot finds and loses the Holy Grail at the Castle of Carbonek. The adventures of Sir Galahad, Sir Percival and Sir Bors and their voyage to Sarras with the Holy Grail. The quest comes to an end.

In the previous tale about Lohengrin we moved ahead many years. We must now return to Sir Lancelot who, on his quest for the Holy Grail, left Percival with the beautiful Blanchefleur, while he set out to find again his son, Galahad.

But Lancelot seemed hounded by ill-luck. He drove his horse over hill and dale, and yet he never caught up with Galahad. Neither did he hear a word about him. Finally, when his horse was at the end of its tether, Sir Lancelot, with much difficulty got himself a new one, and then his adventures began.

One day, he slept in a lonesome spot, and awoke to find his new horse and his sword had disappeared! He had no other choice but to set out again on foot. The countryside was quite deserted now, with no houses or trees, just bare hills.

Lancelot did not know for how many days and nights he walked, hungry and thirsty, but then at last, when his senses were beginning to dim, he came to the sea.

What next? The Knight was well aware that to go back the way he had come was beyond him. So he decided to remain on the shore. "Perhaps a ship may pass by," he consoled himself with a gleam of hope. And, before long, a sail did appear on the horizon

and it grew larger and larger with every minute.

As the vessel came into shallow water, a gangway was lowered and Sir Lancelot embarked. There was not a living soul on board, but what appeared was a table loaded with so many delicious meats and drinks that, without giving a thought to the strange situation, he started eating hungrily.

While he ate the ship began to leave the shore, and when the Knight finished his last drink it was already on the high seas. But Sir Lancelot was not at all concerned; he had placed himself wholly into the hands of fate.

For several days the ship sailed on, always heading in the same direction. And, for all that time, the Knight was at leisure to eat and drink to his heart's content, since the table was always well stocked. The waves played with the ship as if it were a cradle, and not a single cloud appeared in the sky.

Then, one morning, Sir Lancelot saw land. And on the shore was a horseman, carrying a white shield and the shield bore a red cross. The horse started out for the ship. Soon it jumped aboard, and the unknown knight was before him. The knight raised his visor, and it was Sir Galahad! Joyfully he took his father in his arms and started telling his adventures. Neither of them noticed that the shore had, by then, disappeared . . .

"When I left Camelot in quest of the Holy Grail," said Sir Galahad, "there was, as you know, one thing I lacked: a shield. Later, by a marvellous coincidence, I found myself at the White Abbey where I found another Knight of the Round Table, Sir Bagdemagus."

"He is a good fighter," observed Lancelot. "And his son, Meliagrans, does not lack courage either, if only he were more level-headed."

Sir Galahad continued with his story:

. . . Well, it was Sir Bagdemagus who revealed to me that a miraculous shield was being kept in that very abbey, but so far it had brought only bad luck to anyone carrying it.

Even so I was determined to win

205

that shield, but I had to accept Bag-demagus's words: "Should anything happen to me, it shall be yours. But by rights it belongs, first of all, to me."

Then he mounted his horse, and the shield with a large red cross embla-zoned on it was handed to him by his squire. The horse rushed off at such a gallop that Bagdemagus was immedi-ately out of sight. It took his squire three days to find him but when he did, Bagdemagus was badly hurt.

Apparently, the horse had galloped faster and faster. Then, suddenly, Bag-demagus had seen a knight in silver armour with his spear ready to strike. He had tried in vain to protect him-self with the shield, but he could not even raise his hand. So the spear had pierced his shoulder.

When Bagdemagus was brought back upon a litter, he handed over the shield to me, as agreed.

Then I found that I was unable to put my feet into the stirrups properly, so wildly did my horse rear up under me. What followed was a flight, not a ride ... the trees around me were completely blurred, and all I remem-ber is that I nearly knocked over two knights on the way ...

"Sir Percival and myself," interrupt-ed Sir Lancelot. He added with a laugh, "We were both unhorsed, but I recognized you all the same!"

Sir Galahad smiled, then went on with his story:

... Then I saw the knight in silver armour, myself. He stood like a marble statue but there was no sword or spear in his hand. He stopped his horse and said, "That shield is yours by rights, my son; it will guide you towards the Holy Grail until I appear again."

Then he waved to me, his white horse soared from the ground like a bird, and before long he vanished in the clouds... And that was what happened to me before I met you! ...

Such was Sir Galahad's story. Sir Lancelot was very happy to hear that his son had been accorded such an honour. He also had a secret wish that they might reach the Holy Grail together, and at first it looked as if that wish was going to be fulfilled. For weeks and months, their ship sailed over quiet waters, and they always found plenty to eat and drink on the table.

One day, however, a storm suddenly arose, stretching the sails to bursting point. In an instant the ship rose and flew along the crests of the waves, like a bird on the wing. Ragged cliffs appeared on the horizon. Higher and higher the ship rose above the foaming sea until Sir Lancelot felt overcome by faintness.

Before his senses left him completely he heard an unknown voice say, "Follow me, Sir Galahad! But first, bid farewell to your father, for you will never see him again." And in a last flash of consciousness, Sir Lancelot realized that his son was embracing him.

When he recovered, there was no trace of Galahad or the ship, anywhere. Instead, in the distance upon a hill, he saw in the blaze of the setting sun the dark contours of a castle which seemed familiar to him.

Regardless of his tiredness and the pain he felt, he set off towards the

castle. Dusk fell, the night set in, but the moon lit the way until he reached the castle gate. There were two lions acting as sentries. Since the Knight had no weapon, he felt very uneasy indeed. However, the lions just glanced at him, and let him pass into the courtyard.

Sir Lancelot felt his heart throbbing. He entered the tower, ascended a winding staircase and then walked along a dark passage lit by just a few rays of the moon. Even so, he noticed many doors in that passage, but trying to turn their handles, he found them all locked.

He halted at the last one, and the door opened enough to let out a blinding radiance accompanied by tones of heavenly music.

Sir Lancelot entered the chamber without heeding the warning voice which pealed from above. "Flee, Sir Knight, while there is time, since for you the sight of the Holy Grail is forbidden!"

Indeed, the whole room was filled with the radiance of the golden chalice. It stood on a table and was covered with red samite. Sir Lancelot lifted his arm to remove the veil. In the middle of the movement, however, it was as if flames blazed up into his face, and he cried out and collapsed to the floor.

Not even the old books tell whether the Knight was among the living at that moment; the only sure thing is that he lay spiritless for twenty-four days, and only then opened his eyes. He saw the wrinkled face of King Pelles smiling at him with sad kindness, and at that moment Lancelot remembered the fair Elaine.

"She has been dead for a long time now; she died with pining for you," said the old King, as if he were reading Lancelot's thoughts. "That is why you can never achieve the Holy Grail. The only thing you can do is go back. However, hold in high esteem what you have seen here for, to most of your companions, even such good fortune has been denied."

King Pelles gave Lancelot new armour and a new horse, and the Knight left the Castle of Carbonek. Only when he was on his way, did he wonder why he didn't realize what made Carbonek so familiar to him.

Thus ended the quest of the Holy Grail for Sir Lancelot, and we have to say that, up till then, no other Knight of the Round Table had known a similar experience . . .

However, the Knight for whom the

quest of the Holy Grail did not end, was Sir Percival. Having abandoned the lovely Blanchefleur, he rode over hills and dales. He could not even glimpse many of the places he passed because of constant trouble with his horse. His steed was a stubborn stallion and would often run in exactly the opposite direction from that which Percival chose.

One day, towards the evening, he again battled with his horse at some cross-roads. This time the Knight would not give in, but neither would the stallion. And so they might not

have moved from the spot till the morning! But exactly at midnight, Sir Percival heard an alluring female voice say, from behind him, "Would you like to exchange that horse, Sir Knight?"

He turned, and in the light of the moon he saw a lovely lady, all in black, standing at the cross-roads. By the reins, she led a horse who was as black as coal but had fire flaming from his eyes. Percival was delighted to accept the unknown lady's offer without giving a moment's thought to her sudden appearance.

And when the black horse under him began galloping as swift as an arrow, he heard laughter from the cross-roads, so wild that it sent a shiver down his spine. The horse raced on through the dark night, and the horse-man was hard put to it to steer clear of every branch.

After they left the forest, they rushed relentlessly up the hills and down again until the sky began to turn grey before them. Then, the black horse reached a wide river, and at once threw itself into the waters.

At first it swam on the surface but,

when they reached the middle, it suddenly began to submerge. Percival freed one foot from the stirrup, but the other somehow seemed firmly wedged. And while the Knight's head was still above the water, he again heard the wild laughter.

Despite that, the fiendish horse — for it must have been a devil's beast — did not succeed in drowning the Knight. From far behind the hill a cock crowed and Sir Percival was suddenly free. With his last remnants of strength he swam to the surface.

However, the bank was still far off and he would not have reached it but for the knight who appeared there and hastened to his aid.

This was Lancelot's cousin Sir Bors.

He, too, had been led to the river in his quest for the Holy Grail, and when he saw that Percival's strength was giving out, he jumped into the river and pulled him out.

Out of gratitude Percival told him everything, and ended by expressing the wish that they should continue looking for the Holy Grail together.

And this they did. With only one horse between them they travelled slowly but, even so, before noon they reached the sea-shore as Sir Lancelot had done before them.

Sir Percival scanned the ocean and soon caught sight of a mast above the horizon. The ship was approaching fast.

Meanwhile, Sir Bors was watching

ing ship reached the shore, the horseman dismounted and they saw that it was Sir Galahad.

Overjoyed at seeing them again, he greeted his friends of the Round Table and said, "I am destined to take the Holy Grail, in this chest, away from Britain. And since we have met here, I think you have also been chosen for this task."

Without further ado, the Knights loaded the chest on to the ship; then the vessel slid silently from the shore, and out to sea. Very high above them watched a horseman. It was his voice Sir Galahad had heard telling him to bid his father farewell, and it was he who had entrusted the young Knight with the safekeeping of the holy, miraculous chalice . . .

the shore. A knight appeared, riding towards them with a large white shield across his shoulders. In front of his saddle was a wooden chest. As the sail-

The three Knights sailed for many weeks and months, and when the ship reached its destination, they saw the walls of the Babylonian city of Sarras. It was here that the Holy Grail had first appeared and they had been entrusted to return it.

They disembarked, with Percival and Bors carrying the chest and Galahad walking behind them. Not far from the city gate, Galahad saw a bent old man and called to him, "Help us with the chest and we will reward you!"

"I should like to, but for ten years now, being so lame, I have walked only on crutches," answered the old man dejectedly.

Galahad only smiled and said, "But do try! You may manage it now."

And the old man stood up straight and, throwing away his crutches he ran towards them as if he had never been lame. People who were nearby saw the miracle with their own eyes, and at once hurried off to the city with the tale of the three holy Knights who had healed a cripple.

Thus it happened that, even before the Knights reached the city gate, a crowd of sick people had gathered around them. These, too, were cured by Sir Galahad, with the power of the Holy Grail. But while the simple folk began to worship them, the ruler of the city sent his bailiffs to arrest the Knights, and he had them thrown into the deepest dungeon.

The King's name was Estorause. He was a tyrant and his fear now was that his subjects, aided by the unknown Knights, might rise in revolt against

him. So he wanted the Knights to perish in their cold cell.

However, thanks to the Holy Grail, exactly the opposite happened. Although they were imprisoned for nearly a whole year, they came out as healthy as before. Estorause, however, lost strength rapidly and, when he saw that his end was near, he called the Knights to him and asked them to forgive him. This they did, and he passed away in peace.

After the tyrant's death there was no doubt about who was to become the new king. The council of the city of Sarras unanimously chose Sir Galahad and, on the day when they placed the golden crown upon his head, they also opened the chest and set the Holy Grail upon a silver table.

So, the precious cup was there for all. It filled the surroundings with the fragrance and music of Paradise, and Sir Galahad, who knelt nearest to it, was overcome with feelings of absolute peace. It was then that he turned to Sir Bors. "I feel I am not going to stay long in your midst," he announced. "But you must return to Britain and Camelot. Once there, please greet my father, Lancelot, and give him my message that he should, now, give up all the brief pleasures of this world . . ."

Sir Galahad could say no more. To the astonishment of the large congregation, a knight in silver armour, astride a white horse, descended from heaven. He took the young Knight by

the hand, they soared upwards and, before long, both disappeared in the clouds. At that moment, the Holy Grail was lifted by some strange force, to follow Sir Galahad. And that was to be the last time that ordinary mortals would see the holy cup . . .

Such was the end of the quest of the Holy Grail. It only remains to be added that Sir Percival did not stay long in this world, either. He donned a monk's cowl and, with Sir Bors as his faithful companion, he went into seclusion, dying two years later.

Only then did Sir Bors think of returning to the Round Table. He obtained new armour, embarked on a ship at Sarras, and several months later landed on familiar shores.

Hastening to Camelot he rode his

horse at a gallop and, when he rode through the gate, the joy felt by the whole Court is hard to describe, for he had already been given up for dead.

He recounted in every detail the stories of the quest for the Holy Grail, so that King Arthur might have them recorded in a chronicle.

Then, Sir Bors gave Sir Lancelot his son's last message. Lancelot gravely listened to his cousin, embraced him and, to honour Galahad's memory, they pledged each other eternal friendship to the end of their days.

Did they suspect that the time was not far off, when friendship would be needed most of all at the Round Table?

TALE NINETEEN ...
SIR LANCELOT
AND QUEEN
GUINEVERE ...

The last Diamond Tournament and why Queen Guinevere plans a May festival. How she is ambushed by Sir Meliagrans and saved by Sir Lancelot. Sir Lancelot is rescued by the Lady of the Lake and, with Sir Bors and Sir Lionel, he saves Guinevere from burning at the stake. Sir Mordred's deceit. The war between the King and Sir Lancelot and to what end it comes.

Following the return of Sir Bors from the quest of the Holy Grail, Arthur's Knights, somewhat reduced in number, again gathered at the Round Table. The King, and the whole Court with him, was delighted to see them again.

Queen Guinevere was no less pleased to see Sir Lancelot. The two were even more ardently in love than before, but their love was no longer a complete secret. Sir Pelleas still felt hatred for the Knights of the Round Table, and spoke ill of Lancelot and Guinevere wherever he went; and so did Sir Gawain's brothers, Sir Mordred and Sir Agravain.

Lancelot soon learnt about this from his cousin, Sir Bors. He also remembered Sir Galahad's last wish that he should abandon wordly pleasures. For

these reasons Sir Lancelot saw the Queen as little as possible, and he finally left Camelot altogether.

Guinevere, seeing Lancelot's conduct as a betrayal, angrily forbade him access to the Court and went out of her way to bestow more favours on other Knights.

At that time Lancelot took refuge at the manor of Sir Bernard of Astolat — the town we know, today, as Guildford. It was in the colours of Sir Bernard's daughter, who was known as the Fair Maid of Astolat, that he fought in the great tournament held by King Arthur, not long after.

This was the last of the nine Diamond Tournaments of which all the eight had already been won by Sir Lancelot for Guinevere. Yet, this time, he stood against Arthur's Knights. They did not recognize him and puzzled who this magnificent, unknown knight could be.

Such were his achievements in combat that he won the ninth, and largest, diamond. He then rode quickly away. The only person who suspected the knight's true identity was King Arthur, but he kept the suspicion to himself . . .

The angered Queen did not watch the tournament, so she had no inkling as to whether the unknown knight was, in fact, Sir Lancelot. Instead, she called her ten Knights with their ladies, and resolved to hold a May Festival on the meadow at Westminster. It was the custom, in those days, for people of noble birth to don green garments on May Day, and to deck themselves with flowers, to welcome in the Spring.

So, on that day, the Queen rode out; each Knight carried a fair lady behind him, but none was armed.

Sir Meliagrans, son of Sir Bagdemagus, had his castle in Westminster. This rash young man had long felt love for Guinevere and, having heard that Lancelot was absent, he thought up an evil plan. He would carry the Queen off to his castle, and slaughter her unarmed escort.

So he gathered together one hundred and sixty men, including lancers and archers as well as swordsmen. With these he lay in wait on the Queen's route and, when the May procession drew near, Meliagrans gave the order to attack.

It was a very dishonourable fight! In a moment, both horses and knights were rolling on the ground, and among those of the Queen's Knights who received the most blows were Sir Kay, Sir Agravain and Sir Pelleas.

However, on seeing Meliagrans, Guinevere at once guessed his intentions. In a flash she tore the emerald ring from her finger and, handing it to her squire who had miraculously been preserved from the blows, she whispered, "Take this ring to Sir Lancelot of the Lake and beg him to come and save me!"

Without hesitation the boy spurred his horse, bent his head over the mane, and rushed off at lightning speed. Though pursued and shot at, he escaped, and so Sir Lancelot received the news of the Queen's danger that very morning. He had his steed saddled and, armed to the teeth, he dashed off to Westminster.

However, Meliagrans had guessed the squire's destination, and so he placed guards along the road to delay Sir Lancelot. Meanwhile, the Queen and her escort were taken to Meliagrans' castle. Nearly all Guinevere's Knights had suffered injury, but fortunately none had been killed.

Late in the afternoon, Sir Lancelot arrived near the spot where the attack had taken place. Arrows came hurtling through the air. "Just shoot to your hearts' content," the Knight laughed at the hidden archers. "My armour and shield give me good protection!"

Sadly, however, they shot his defenceless horse from under him. Neighing, the white horse tumbled, and when Sir Lancelot had disentangled himself from the stirrups he cried angrily, "Come closer, you cowards, so that I can cross swords with you! I can see you prefer swooping upon travellers, like robbers, rather

222

than standing up to them!" However, the only reply was the pounding of departing horses.

Sir Lancelot had to continue his journey on foot, burdened by his heavy armour and weapons. Before long he was fortunate enough to meet a carter who carried him, in his cart, to Meliagrans' castle. This, later, led to Sir Lancelot being called the Knight of the Cart.

Meliagrans looked out of the castle window and, to his horror, saw the Queen's protector. The blood froze in his veins. Well aware that his life hung in the balance, he ran to Guinevere, went down on his knees, and pleaded, "I beg for mercy, Your Majesty. I will put right every evil I have done, only plead for me with Lancelot to spare my life."

By then, Lancelot was knocking at the gate and shouting, "Come out, you coward, so that I can punish you!"

"Why so much anger, Sir Knight?" spoke the Queen. "Calm down and come inside in peace, for Sir Meliagrans is repentant of what he has done."

Sir Lancelot was dumbfounded, and entered the castle as calm as a lamb. As for Meliagrans, he behaved as if truly penitent, but in his heart a desire for revenge was simmering. He would just wait for his opportunity!

The Queen, with Sir Lancelot and the other Knights of the Round Table, were entertained with a rich dinner, and Sir Lancelot urged the others to make their peace with Meliagrans.

But Lancelot wished to be alone with Guinevere, so the two agreed in secret that he would come to her chamber that night. The eleventh hour struck, then midnight too passed, and Lancelot started out along the dark corridor. He trod as silently as he could, but even so he was watched by Meliagrans.

trap-door, laughed vengefully, and crept back to his chamber.

The next morning Sir Lancelot was missed, but since he often left unexpectedly, no one but Guinevere was surprised.

On the other hand, Meliagrans was highly delighted. He had the injuries, suffered by the Knights, tended and even offered protection to the Queen on her return journey to Camelot. However, he was hatching another plot in his mind . . .

Having found out that Gawain's brothers, Agravain and Mordred, were living at Camelot, Meliagrans called on them and said, "I have brought the King important information about the Queen and Sir Lancelot. In fact, I saw Lancelot enter her chamber after midnight, and as I was about to stop him, sword in hand, he took fright and fled. He was not to be found this morning, and he did not come back to Camelot!"

Particularly for Sir Mordred, the Knight with the foxy face, the slanderous words were music to the ears and he searched for Sir Gawain to let him into the secret.

"I am not sure if we should believe what he says," said Sir Gawain, when he was told. "Since this would surely bring about a rift, if not a war, between the King and the Knight of the Lake. For the sake of the brotherhood of the Knights of the Round Table, this must not happen!"

Sir Lancelot was about to take the last step to the Queen's chamber, when the floor suddenly opened beneath him and, with a cry, he fell deep into a dungeon. His cry was not heard and Meliagrans, who had set the

224

"But I think the King should learn everything! You surely agree he must not be allowed to suffer such dishonour . . ." Mordred started shouting.

Before Sir Gawain could stem Mordred's words, Arthur himself entered the room and demanded, "Why all this uproar? What should I learn of?"

"Sire," replied Sir Agravain, "we have to inform you that Lancelot of the Lake is a traitor. There is an affair of love between him and the Queen, but you believe him to be your best friend. Let Sir Meliagrans tell what he has witnessed, so that you may become convinced!"

After King Arthur had listened to Meliagrans' slanderous speech, he buried his head in his hands. When be raised his eyes again, his face was burning with anger. "They will both be punished for such treachery," he cried. "I will send men-at-arms to search for Lancelot, and the Queen shall be burnt at the stake! You, Sir Gawain, will escort her to her execution."

But the Knight replied, "I have no wish to look upon so shameful an end of that noble lady, and I do not agree with what you propose. Why not wait at least until Sir Lancelot appears and we can find the truth of the matter?"

Arthur was a just man and he might well have heeded Gawain's words but for Sir Mordred, who launched into a malicious tirade.

So, on that very same day, the poor Queen was stripped of her finery and, wearing only a simple shirt, she was locked in the dungeon beneath the main tower where she awaited her death.

225

he expected to see entered the jail. It was the Lady of the Lake.

"Yes, it is I, Lancelot," she smiled. Her lovely face had not changed since the day when the Knight — still a young lad at the time — last saw her in her lake kingdom. "I have come to help you, because the Queen finds herself in mortal peril," she went on.

When she had recounted all that had happened at Camelot, Lancelot just groaned, "Oh, those villains! But I will show them, all of them! Just you wait!"

"They deserve nothing better," agreed the Lady of the Lake. "But you must not weaken your friendship with the King, or you will bring down ruin on the entire Round Table. Remember that!"

So Sir Lancelot vowed that he would not stand against Arthur and, only then, the Lady of the Lake led him out of the dungeon and gave him armour and a new horse. It was the finest white horse that the Knight had ever possessed. Hardly had he sunk into the saddle than the steed ran like the wind, straight towards Camelot.

Lancelot had not ridden far when he suddenly heard the clatter of horses' hooves, and a group of riders armed to the teeth rushed at him out of the forest. Among them were Sir Bors, Sir Lionel and a number of other friends. But, instead of greeting Sir Lancelot, they all lowered their visors and drew their swords.

All that time, Sir Lancelot lay on the floor of his prison, thinking that Meliagrans was out to torture him to death with hunger and thirst. Eventually, however, he heard the clatter of keys. The door opened and the last person

"Hold!" cried Sir Lancelot. "You must listen to me, for you have been deceived!" Unwillingly, they sheathed their weapons, but they still surrounded him.

"No doubt you know why we are seeking you," cried Sir Bors. "Unless you convince us of your innocence, you shall go to the stake along with the Queen!"

Lancelot looked him straight in the eyes and answered, "By our brotherhood I swear that the traitor is Meliagrans. It was he who captured the Queen during the May Festival . . ."

When he had finished the account of what had really happened and how he was freed from the dungeon by the Lady of the Lake, Sir Bors exclaimed, "Quickly to Camelot to save the Queen!"

They urged their horses on until they reached the familiar walls. The gate was wide open and, in the courtyard, they could see a large stake. At that very moment the Queen, deathly pale, and in her flaxen shirt, was being led towards it.

"Wait, she is innocent!" cried Sir Lancelot from afar. But his enemies, Sir Mordred, Sir Agravain and especially Sir Meliagrans, raised a cry: "Kill the traitor! To arms!" they shouted. The confusion and fracas which followed is extremely hard to describe. Sir Lancelot and his companions wanted only to save Guinevere and to give the three conspirators

a sound thrashing. But at the call to arms, Sir Gawain's brothers, Sir Gaheris and Sir Gareth, drew their swords, and the other Knights followed suit.

Sir Lancelot himself performed wonders with his own sword. With

227

one stroke he smashed the stake, and with another he delivered the Queen from her shameful fetters. He then dealt Meliagrans such a blow that the traitor's arm flew away together with his shoulder, and his blood gushed in all directions.

Then Sir Lancelot saw that Sir Agravain was charging to run him through with his lance. He spurred his horse until the animal reared up and he was high above the battlefield. From the saddle Lancelot used his shield to strike his attacker's skull, driving it between his shoulder-blades.

No lesser feats of prowess were performed by Sir Lancelot's companions, especially Sir Bors and Sir Lionel. Meanwhile, Lancelot had felled Sir Gareth and Sir Gaheris without ever recognizing them and, sword in hand, was guarding the entrance to the tower so that the Queen could dress.

Soon, there was not a single Knight left in the courtyard, willing to oppose him. Lancelot sat Guinevere on his white steed and he and his friends set off for his Castle of the Joyous Gard. Today, some think this was at Bamburgh, others that it was at Alnwick.

He had no regrets; the only thing that troubled him was that in the courtyard he had not killed the artful Mordred, him of the foxy face.

Mordred, in fact, in his bloodthirsty way, had waited around to see the Queen burnt, unlike the King and all the good Knights, such as Sir Gawain, Sir Kay the Seneschal, Sir Lucas and Sir Bedivere who sat, sad and dejected, at the Round Table. However, when the terrible carnage started, Mordred hid behind a tree and did not stick out his nose from his hiding-place until Lancelot was gone.

Then he ran to King Arthur to describe to him how the Knight of the Lake had robbed him of his Queen and how he had mercilessly slain so many Knights of the Round Table; and all for the sake of his sinful love. The King addressed his remaining Knights in a broken voice. "This is our ruin. I do not wonder at him, being a good Knight, wishing to save the Queen. For indeed, we ourselves chose to sit here rather than to watch her die. But when I learn that Gaheris and Gareth are dead . . ."

"Poor Beaumains . . . the man who loved Lancelot more than anyone else!" exclaimed Sir Gawain. "For that, I shall never forgive Lancelot." He went on, "And you, Sire, must declare war on him, even if he should flee to Benwick!"

Arthur just shook his head sadly. Then he said, "I believe we shall find

him at the Castle of the Joyous Gard. And if you will not forgive him, then neither can I. So let us call together an expedition without delay!"

So the King sent out letters all over the realm, trying to gather together a great army as soon as possible. Sir Lancelot, also, wasted no time. He managed to get together large numbers of good men-at-arms, when he explained who had really been responsible for the feud.

All the same, the King's armies were greatly superior in numbers, so Lancelot chose to remain in his castle, while Arthur laid siege to it.

The siege dragged on for fifteen weeks, without either side making a decisive attack. During that time Sir Lancelot spoke with the King several times, from a window, giving him proof of the Queen's innocence as well as of his own. Had it not been for Sir Gawain's insistence, they would have surely come to terms. But Arthur's nephew, wishing to avenge the death of his brothers at any price, incited everyone to fight.

When the battle finally took place, it was not a glorious one for the royal side. At its very outset, Sir Bors threw Arthur from his horse. He might have killed the King had not Sir Lancelot forbidden this and helped Arthur to remount.

Then, Sir Gawain killed Sir Lionel with his lance but immediately after that he sustained such an injury that he had to be carried from the battlefield on a litter.

After that, Lancelot's army carried the day, since there was no Knight in the royal army willing to incite further fighting, as Gawain had done. So the King ordered a retreat and Lancelot chose not to pursue him.

Meanwhile, the news of the unfortunate feud concerning the Queen had spread throughout the world. However, Sir Lancelot and the King, together with many of the rest of the Knights, sorely regretted having allowed themselves to be inveigled into war.

And then, one day, Camelot saw a magnificent procession. Exactly one hundred of Sir Lancelot's knights, all clad in green and each carrying an olive branch as a token of peace, walked accompanying twenty-four high-born ladies of the Queen's retinue. Leading the procession were the Knight of the Lake and Guinevere, both clad in white, gold-embroidered gowns, and they went down on their knees in front of the royal throne upon which Arthur was seated.

Lancelot delivered up the Queen according to custom. Once again he pleaded her innocence and, in the sight of all, gave her a last, warm kiss. Then she took her place beside King Arthur.

Sir Lancelot made a farewell speech saying, "Sire, I depart for Benwick, because I wish to find again grace and friendship in your heart, as in the days when we were helping each other. It is also my wish that the glory of your Round Table may never die!"

King Arthur just nodded in agreement — overcome with emotion. There were many others, too, whose eyes filled with tears, and there was loud crying and sobbing as Sir Lancelot left the banqueting hall.

In the doorway, however, stood a Knight. He addressed Sir Lancelot with quite a different emotion. "Let the King do whatever he may think fit. But I, because of my brothers' deaths, will never become reconciled with you as long as I live!"

And that Knight was Sir Gawain.

TALE TWENTY . . .
THE DEATH
OF ARTHUR . . .

King Arthur's war expedition to Benwick and Sir Gawain's duels with Lancelot. Sir Mordred's treachery. The death of Sir Gawain. The disastrous battle in Cornwall. The death of Arthur and the lamentable end of the heroes of the Round Table.

Having left Britain, Sir Lancelot set out for his overseas kingdom, taking with him his cousin, Sir Bors, and a number of the other Knights of the Round Table, not previously mentioned in these tales.

Upon reaching Benwick, the Knight of the Lake put the affairs of his realm in order, rewarded all those who had rendered him faithful service, and looked forward to leading a peaceful and quiet life.

This, however, was not to be granted to him. For meanwhile Sir Gawain, in league with Sir Mordred, had persuaded the King that the offences and wrongs inflicted upon them by Lancelot should not go unpunished and that he should prepare a war expedition.

By then Arthur was no longer young and he did not feel like going into battle again. But the two Knights were insistent and so he mustered an army

of sixty thousand fighting men. He then charged Sir Mordred with administering the country, committed Guinevere to his care, and embarked at Southampton with his army.

No sooner had the royal vessel left the shore and the wind filled her sails, than King Arthur slept and had a strange dream. High in the air he saw a giant bear fighting with a dragon. The dragon was under constant attack until, at last, it knocked its opponent down. Thereupon the bear reared up . . . but Arthur did not learn the outcome, for he awoke at that very moment.

Nevertheless, he hoped the dream prophesied his winning a war against Lancelot since, as at all times, the King's banner bore the sign of a dragon.

No sooner had they landed in France than Arthur's men-at-arms set about pillaging and ravaging Sir Lancelot's lands. They made a rapid advance towards Benwick.

Sir Lancelot, remembering the pledge he had made at Camelot, did not march against Arthur. All he did was to order his armies and his people to safe positions behind the fortified bastions of towns or castles, and he then sent the King an offer of truce.

However, just as before, Gawain dissuaded Arthur from accepting a truce. And so the King's army laid siege to Benwick and set ladders against its walls.

Yet not a single man crossed the walls. With little harm to themselves, Sir Lancelot's men kept out the besiegers and reduced their numbers considerably.

Then Sir Gawain, armed to the teeth, rode up to the gate and cried,

"Lancelot, where are you? Do you expect others to fight for you on the walls? Come out and duel with me and prove you are not a cowardly braggart!"

Before long the gate opened and Sir Lancelot, also in full armour, rode out on his white horse.

The duel began with such a force that, at the very first charge, the Knights broke their spears against each other's shield, and both their horses fell. Having disentangled themselves, the Knights drew their swords.

Now Sir Gawain went into the attack and, for no less than three hours, the Knight of the Lake was hard put to it to ward off Sir Gawain's heavy sword. But then, Lancelot seized the weapon with both hands and struck such a blow to his opponent's helmet that Gawain fell, and was unable to rise again. Sir Lancelot stepped aside.

"Why do you not finish me off, traitor?" shrieked the powerless Gawain. "Believe me, when my wound is healed we shall take the field again, and then I will kill you!"

"Maybe I shall last through that battle as well," responded Lancelot with no hatred in his voice and, without looking back, he walked slowly into the town.

In three weeks, Sir Gawain's wound had healed well. He reappeared in the meadow under the walls, once again in full armour, and challenged Sir Lancelot to another duel. . .

This time Gawain's attacks were

even more savage. But for the shield which the Knight of the Lake wielded so expertly, he would certainly have been hacked to pieces.

And, just as before, it took three hours for their strengths to become equalized. Then Lancelot charged. Pieces flew off from Gawain's shield until it split altogether, and Lancelot's sword found the same mark that it found in the previous encounter.

Sir Gawain fainted with pain but, before Sir Lancelot had reached the town gate, he recovered and shouted,

"God knows you shall not escape from me a third time! So prepare yourself once more, since you lack the courage to slay me!"

Lancelot did not answer; he merely nodded. Then he ordered his guards to let him know, without fail, if Sir Gawain should appear for a third time.

The unavailing siege continued. Nearly a month passed and Sir Gawain had not, as yet, shown himself.

Then, one day early in the morning, the besieged people of Benwick saw a strange sight. Amidst great commo-

235

tion, the besiegers had taken down their tents and, down to the last man, were moving off with all speed.

Sir Lancelot found it hard to believe that King Arthur or Sir Gawain would be leaving the field in such a manner. However, this really was the case, and there was good reason for it. . .

What had happened was that, in that early morning, with Sir Gawain sitting in Arthur's tent getting ready for another duel, a breathless messenger came in riding from the shore. "Sire," he said, "while you and your army are here in a foreign country, Sir Mordred has seized your crown . . . He forged letters which said that you were dead, and many noblemen have come to believe that. He even tried to marry Queen Guinevere, but she escaped to the Tower of London where she is being protected by faithful friends. And, God willing, they will protect her until you yourself arrive!"

The news was so dreadful that none of those present would, at first, believe it. Then, after a while, the King put his arm around the messenger and said to him, "I believe you." Then he turned to the others and continued, "Now I can see clearly why Mordred urged us so eagerly to go and fight Lancelot. It has, for a long time, been his intention to break the brotherhood of the Round Table and to rule Britain himself. Now, thanks to our actions, he has nearly succeeded. But he will pay dearly for his treachery!"

Sir Gawain broke the silence that followed. "I know that, because of the

hatred I felt, I am responsible for what has happened," he said. "However, even I can see now who the real villain is. Therefore I will help you, Sire, with all my heart."

Following Gawain, all the other Knights in the camp pledged their faith to the King and, before long, their ships were heading for Dover.

A bloody battle awaited them, for Mordred, having been warned of Arthur's arrival, intended to prevent him from landing.

When his men-at-arms had managed to reach the shore, Arthur sent his foot soldiers to carry out the main assault. Meanwhile, Knights on horseback attacked the enemy's rear on both flanks, and wrought vengeance on them without mercy. So, step by step, the royal army gained the field.

Before long, Sir Mordred was forced to retreat. But many of Arthur's Knights had died upon that battlefield. Then, Sir Gawain was found. He was lying in a barge, and he was dying.

As the King knelt down beside him, his friend and companion of the Round Table spoke to him for the last time. "Sire," he said, "I am dying. In the fight, the wounds I received at Benwick reopened. . . Please give this letter to Sir Lancelot," and he pulled from his armour a parchment scroll. Then, with his voice weakening, Sir Gawain continued, "In the letter I beg him to forgive me and to help you in your struggle. I have sealed it with my

own blood. . ." Then the head of the dying man sank limply into the King's arms, and the brave Knight was silent for ever.

Cornwall and there, by the River Camel, he halted his army to get ready for the decisive battle. When the King arrived there, sixty thousand rebels stood like a mighty wall against him.

This did not frighten Arthur and, as evening drew near, he realized that there would be no fighting until the next day. So he had a camp built and guards set, and then lay down for a brief rest in his tent.

The pursuit of Mordred had made him very weary, and he soon fell asleep. Again, he had a strange dream. In that dream Sir Gawain entered his tent, sat down at his bedside and spoke to him, "Sire," he said, "do not allow the battle to take place tomorrow, or much blood will flow and it will be a disastrous fight for you. Instead, talk with Mordred and wait until Lancelot comes to your aid. His ships are ready. . ."

The Knight's ghost said no more. He dissolved like mist, and the King opened his eyes. The tent was quite empty, but Arthur took the words of his dead companion to heart.

That very evening he sent messengers to ask Sir Mordred to negotiate. Mordred was afraid of an attack by the King, so he was pleased at the idea of a parley, to discuss terms.

The two sides agreed upon a single condition. During the parley no man must draw a bare sword, or that would be taken as the sign for battle to commence.

However, the fighting was not yet over. Arthur resolutely pursued the self-appointed ruler who took refuge behind the walls of a town, hoping he would not be driven out from there. But the town was stormed, and once again Mordred had to make his cowardly escape.

This time he fled westwards into

The old books tell that, on the following morning, the King and Sir Mordred met for their parley. It was held in the middle of the field between the two armies, and each leader brought with him fourteen knights, as agreed. Arthur wanted to avoid battle, so he promised his foxy-faced nephew the rule over Cornwall as well as Kent.

Mordred was astounded by such magnanimity. Without trying to hide his delight he gave the order for cups to be filled with wine.

And then a certain knight — no one knows to which side he belonged — stepped on an adder upon the moor and was stung by it; and so, in an attempt to kill the snake, he drew his sword.

But the glitter of the weapon was seen by both armies. As if by command, the war trumpets, horns and bugles were sounded, and the two armies rushed against each another.

Both Arthur and Mordred at once returned to their own faithful followers, and then a cruel and merciless carnage followed. There were hundreds of dead, but neither side was willing to give way. Arthur, himself, fought as gallantly as in his young days and, where his standard streamed, there the fighting was heaviest.

For the whole day the battle continued and, as the sun sank in the west, Mordred all alone stood behind a wall of dead and wounded.

Arthur was mad with rage and sor-

row, for an enormous number of his own Knights, too, lay dead on the battlefield. Ignoring the warnings of Sir Bedivere and Sir Lucas the Butler, the King charged at the traitor with his lance, and dealt him a mortal blow.

Perhaps it was his anger that had made Arthur forget all about his miraculous sword Excalibur. And perhaps

The King was carried from the battle-field by Sir Bedivere, who prayed fervently that Arthur would, once more, open his eyes. In a few moments his prayer was answered, but Arthur's words brought only pain. "I must ask you to render me one last service," said the wounded King. "Unbuckle my sword, Excalibur, and throw it into the water, and then come to me and tell me what you have seen. . ."

However, Sir Bedivere still hoped for the King's recovery, so he hid the weapon under a tree. He returned to Arthur, and said, "Sire, I saw nothing but the waves and the wind."

The King sighed sadly, and asked him, again, to throw Excalibur into the water. For the second time Sir Bedivere disobeyed, and when the wounded King asked him what he had seen, he was embarrassed and answered, "Nothing, Sire, only the waves lapping and growing dark."

"You lie!" exclaimed Arthur. "And remember this: unless you fulfil my order, I shall be the one to suffer."

Only then did Bedivere take the sword and, winding the belt round the hilt, he threw it into the water. At that moment the familiar slender hand, clothed in white samite appeared above the surface. It caught the sword and brandished it three times, and then the hand and the sword disappeared into the depths.

Sir Bedivere, out of breath, recounted what he had seen. The King heard

it was a similar anger in the dying Mordred that gave him the strength to raise himself once more, and he dealt the King a heavy blow.

Then Mordred breathed his last.

him to the end, then he took his faithful Knight by the hand, and said, "It is time to say goodbye. Just carry me to the shore, but quickly so that I may not miss the barge."

No sooner had Sir Bedivere, with the dying King in his arms, reached the shore than a black barge appeared on the horizon. It came closer and closer to the shore and, when it stopped in front of the Knight, he saw on board three beautiful, sad maidens clad in black robes.

One of them assisted in placing Arthur's body in the barge, and she was the Lady of the Lake. The barge moved away from the shore. The soft rustle of the waves mingled with the

wailing of the maidens. Sir Bedivere could scarcely distinguish his King's last words: "Let no one mourn me; I am departing for the happy Isle of Avalon, where all my wounds shall be healed forever."

And so, King Arthur passed from this world...

All that remains to be added is what happened to the Queen and Sir Lancelot. As soon as Guinevere learnt about the terrible battle and that the King was slain, she mourned greatly and took the veil. From then on, she could not be cheered by anyone, not even Sir Lancelot. He had come too late to the

King's aid and, instead of the expected battle, he heard only the tragic news.

When he finally found the Queen she wept bitterly, blaming herself for having loved him, because this had led to the ruin of the brotherhood of the Round Table. Then she bade Sir Lancelot farewell for ever, and they parted without even a last kiss.

After that, Sir Lancelot lost all interest in the affairs of the world and retired, in solitude, to his Castle of the Joyous Gard.

However, there was one more service that he could render Guinevere, but it was a sad one, indeed. News came to Sir Lancelot that the Queen had died at the nunnery, and he escorted her funeral procession to Glastonbury, where she was given a magnificent funeral.

Before long, Sir Lancelot's own life's candle burnt out. According to his wish, his body was laid to eternal rest at the Castle of the Joyous Gard, for it was there that he had experienced more joys and sorrows than in his native Benwick. . .

The death of Sir Lancelot brought to an end the glorious adventures of the Knights of the Round Table. But the stories of their exploits have lived on, and so the Knights live on — in the memory — along with their beloved King, Arthur — REX QUONDAM REXQUE FUTURUS.

TALE TWENTY ONE
. . . AND THE LAST

Arthur — real and literary. The education of knights and their life. In brief, a tale dedicated to the young reader by way of an explanation and a farewell.

Once King — King for all time . . . that is, perhaps, how the last words of the tale about the brave Arthur and his Knights may best be interpreted.

Some fourteen centuries have passed since the time when Arthur actually lived and defended — probably as one of the chieftains of the Celtic tribes — the south-western part of Britain against the Saxons. Since then, his adventures have fired the imagination of minstrels, poets and writers, and fascinated listeners and readers alike.

In fact, the legend has been very much a developing one. Each author, over the centuries, was influenced by the ideas of his or her own time. This has resulted in not only many contradictions and ambiguities, but also a 'time warp' into the medieval period!

Thousands and thousands of pages have been written about the Knights of the Round Table. The author of this book selected those adventures which he considered the most important and of the most interest to young readers.

The first man to acquaint the world

with King Arthur and his Knights was Galfridus Monemutensis, Geoffrey of Monmouth. In his *History of the Kings of Britain* (in Latin, *Historia Regum Britanniae),* completed in 1136, he included both real figures and events and entirely fictitious ones. Geoffrey made King Arthur a romantic hero. He is likely to have been influenced by popular legends, and perhaps some of the previous chronicles, especially those of the ninth-century Nennius. However, even so, the credit for the fact that, before long, Arthur shared popularity as a heroic figure in feudal Europe with Alexander of Macedonia and Charlemagne, belongs to Geoffrey of Monmouth.

The poets of Continental Europe developed the Arthurian theme. They drew, also, on the verses of the old bards of French Bretagne. This area was known as 'Little Britain' and had been populated by Celts, driven out of Britain by the Saxons. Their legends tended to concentrate on magic happenings. Later, the tales were known as *The Mabinogion*, where the word 'mabinogi' means 'instruction for young bards'. And, in the fourteenth century, they were collected together in a Welsh manuscript known as the *Red Book of Hergest*, which is held, today, in the Library of Jesus College, Oxford.

Meanwhile, in the late twelfth century, the French poetess Marie de France, wrote stories in verse, some of which featured King Arthur and Sir Tristram. And another French writer, Chrétien de Troyes, wrote courtly romances for the aristocracy. Included among these was *The Knight of the Cart*, and this introduced Sir Lancelot as a chivalrous warrior who loved and protected noble women and who defended the Christian faith.

In the same spirit of chivalry, many books and poems were written by authors from the various countries of Europe. For example, *Parzifal* by Wolfram von Eschenbach was all about Sir Percival and the Holy Grail and there were many versions of the story of Tristram and Isolde.

Interest in the Arthurian stories was revived in Britain when William Caxton printed, in twenty-one volumes, the most comprehensive collection of both historical and romantic stories ever, entitled *Le Morte d'Arthur* (in English, this means 'The Death of Arthur'), which was completed by Thomas Malory in about 1469.

Malory admitted that he had used French sources, but he did, also, greatly enrich the stories.

Le Morte d'Arthur was to inspire, later, such famous English poets as Spenser, Milton, Wordsworth and Tennyson. Many young readers will, already, have come across Tennyson's *Idylls of the King*, which deal chiefly with the bad behaviour of the Knights that led to the ruin of the Round Table. And, at about the same time,

Mark Twain wrote his satirical story, *A Connecticut Yankee in King Arthur's Court*, in which he attacked both the past and the, then, present.

Today, as well as literary works, we have operas, music and films based on the legends and — developing with the times — even computer games and theme parks!

Readers may also be interested to learn that King Arthur is kept very much alive by the *Arthurian Society*, which has members in thirty countries of the world.

To help young readers to better understand the tales we have just told, let us add a brief description of what a knight's education and life in the Middle Ages was really like.

As a rule, the home and the symbol of a feudal ruler was his stone castle. Usually this was built, for reasons of defence, on a high and not easily accessible site, later to be surrounded by walls and often by a moat. The whole building was constructed around a square tower (which became rounded from the thirteenth century onwards) where the most significant events — such as court sessions and banquets — took place. In the main hall, there were tables and two seats on a dais for the lord of the castle and his consort or for a distinguished guest. Otherwise, until the thirteenth century, people sat on furs. There were other rooms in the tower, and the ground floor usually housed the granaries.

Life in the castle was run by a body of servants chosen from among the lord's subjects; their number was determined by the wealth of the feudal lord, and there were noblemen's courts even more magnificent than the royal court, which was the one the lords tried to emulate. And so, apart from ladies of the castle (the female retinue, as they were called) and the pages and squires, who were of noble descent, there were huntsmen, grooms, butlers, guards, and kitchen and other staff. The most important office was held by the castle warden (the castellan, burgrave) who both managed the whole economy of the castle and generally supervised the upbringing and education of future feudal lords.

This education was designed to ensure the prowess of members of the very small ruling group in all respects and, for this reason, it was long, very exacting and rigid. The unwritten knightly code of honour also prescribed, in no uncertain terms, absolute obedience to the Church and its protection, respect for feudal rights and duties, and fighting to the death against everything that endangered these, and also the defence of truth against lies and injustice, respect for women (but only the high-born ladies, of course) and defence of the weak.

Up to his seventh year, a nobleman's son would remain at home, for the most part in the care of women. By then, however, he already knew how to ride a horse and how to play chess. After this he would go 'for tuition' to another feudal lord, of as high standing as possible. If he were very fortunate, he would go to the King himself. Then his education was chiefly in the hands of men.

Anyone aspiring to knighthood was called up to his fourteenth year 'a page' and was expected to know how to read and write, to master the elements of mathematics, music, the making of arms, at least one foreign language and, of course, Christian doctrine.

In their physical education, pages were trained, primarily, in the use of arms and hunting. They learnt how to wield the sword, the spear, the lance, and even the battle-axe. They were taught horse riding and the care of horses. The art of hunting consisted mainly of archery and the chase. In some places falconry was preferred, although conventional deer hunting was generally regarded as more manly. As well as this, the pages would serve at the feudal lord's table, learn to dance and to play the harp or the lute.

At the age of fourteen a page would become a squire. From then on the knightly training continued in heavy armour and squires would accompany their lord both to tournaments and on war expeditions. Since noble-born maidens were also being educated in the castle, each squire would select one, upon whom he centred all his wishes and desires, whether in words and songs or in deeds of prowess. For this reason, the virtues of a squire, held in highest esteem, were courage and high-spiritedness, courtesy and gallantry towards ladies. Of course, both squires and young knights would often 'steal' each other's ladies, and their jealousy could lead to wild and deadly skirmishes.

The age of entry into the order of knighthood, called dubbing, varied, starting from as early as fifteen years. Dubbing of knights was mainly performed at Eastertide and Pentecost, at weddings or christening parties, and after victorious battles. The ceremonies were accompanied by tournaments and feasting. Every knight had the right to dub, but this right was most frequently used by the high aristocracy and by the King.

The principal rite was girting with a sword and a symbolic blow with the back of the hand on to the bare neck of the squire being dubbed. But sometimes, as recorded in old chronicles, these blows were heavier than expected, particularly if the young man was being dubbed by his own father!

It would appear that, after being dubbed, the young knight was expected to marry a noble and beautiful maiden and, after the wedding, to lead a life full of adventure on the fields of battle and at tournaments and hunts.

As a rule, reality was different. Any

feudal lord was continually involved in disputes with his subjects who were forced to work in his fields, pay him dues, and serve in his army as well. There were, also, quarrels with other nobles, the King or the Church who, like him, were trying to accumulate as much wealth and property as possible.

All this led not only to armed skirmishes, but also to marriages of convenience, where by far the main consideration was property, not the bride's beauty and purity. Indeed, even the romantic love of the brave Sir Lancelot and Queen Guinevere is questioned by some literary historians. They point out that, since Lancelot was not born until the time of Guinevere's marriage to Arthur, he was hardly likely to have fallen in love with a Queen some fifteen years his senior.

Participation in battles was not likely to have been a pleasant experience. A feudal lord's duty was to give assistance in battle to the King, or, in the case of the lower gentry, to a knight of a higher status. Many a war expedition meant a year or even several years away from one's own estate, which no one really welcomed.

On the actual battlefield, a knight would fight as well as he could. For one thing, he did not want to be killed, and for another he hoped to gain a share of the war booty as his reward. For some, be they kings or robber knights, warfare became their whole life . . .

Let us now explain a little about knightly tournaments. These became very popular, particularly in Western Europe. They were somewhat like battles, but in small sporting editions. During a tournament, a knight was able to prove his physical fitness, his horsemanship and his warrior prowess, without inflicting a serious injury on his opponent. And, in time, certain rules became established which reduced injuries even more; for example a ban on weapons with sharp points.

The victor was usually the contestant who showed the greatest prowess in every respect. This might be the knight who remained longest in the saddle, dealt the greatest number of blows, or was the last to lift his visor. However, the choice was also affected by the personal feelings of the noble ladies and maidens who acted as judges.

In conclusion, let us say that, in the tales we have told in this book, our aim has been to acquaint young readers with an important and fascinating example of medieval literature. Of course, there are many contradictions between the legend and the reality. Very young readers will accept them as quite normal in stories of magic and adventure. Older readers will, we are sure, understand that — with legends that have developed over the centuries — such contradictions are inevitable. Above all, we hope the tales have given you pleasure and enjoyment.